Elder Smith

The poetical works of Robert Browning

Vol. X

Elder Smith

The poetical works of Robert Browning
Vol. X

ISBN/EAN: 9783742842831

Manufactured in Europe, USA, Canada, Australia, Japa

Cover: Foto ©Andreas Hilbeck / pixelio.de

Manufactured and distributed by brebook publishing software
(www.brebook.com)

Elder Smith

The poetical works of Robert Browning

Ritratto dell'infelice Guido Franceschini

il quale fu decapitato in Roma alli 22 febbraio 1698.

Engraved by G. book, from a Drawing made on the day of Guido's execution

London Published by Smith Elder & Cº 15 Waterloo Place

THE POETICAL WORKS

of

ROBERT BROWNING

VOL. X.

THE RING AND THE BOOK, VOL. III.

LONDON
SMITH, ELDER, & CO., 15 WATERLOO PLACE
1889

CONTENTS.

THE RING AND THE BOOK.

1868-9.

IX.

JURIS DOCTOR JOHANNES-BAPTISTA BOTTINIUS,

FISCI ET REV. CAM. APOSTOL. ADVOCATUS.

HAD I God's leave, how I would alter things!
If I might read instead of print my speech,—
Ay, and enliven speech with many a flower
Refuses obstinate to blow in print,
As wildings planted in a prim parterre,—   5
This scurvy room were turned an immense hall;
Opposite, fifty judges in a row;
This side and that of me, for audience—Rome:
And, where yon window is, the Pope should hide—
Watch, curtained, but peep visibly enough.   10
A buzz of expectation! Through the crowd,

x.   ʙ

Jingling his chain and stumping with his staff,
Up comes an usher, louts him low, "The Court
"Requires the allocution of the Fisc!"
I rise, I bend, I look about me, pause   15
O'er the hushed multitude: I count—One, two——

Have ye seen, Judges, have ye, lights of law,—
When it may hap some painter, much in vogue
Throughout our city nutritive of arts,
Ye summon to a task shall test his worth,   20
To manufacture, as he knows and can,
A work may decorate a palace-wall,
Afford my lords their Holy Family,—
Hath it escaped the acumen of the Court
How such a painter sets himself to paint?   25
Suppose that Joseph, Mary and her Babe
A-journeying to Egypt, prove the piece:
Why, first he sedulously practiseth,
This painter,—girding loin and lighting lamp,—
On what may nourish eye, make facile hand;   30
Getteth him studies (styled by draughtsmen so)
From some assistant corpse of Jew or Turk
Or, haply, Molinist, he cuts and carves,—
This Luca or this Carlo or the like.
To him the bones their inmost secret yield,   35

Each notch and nodule signify their use :
On him the muscles turn, in triple tier,
And pleasantly entreat the entrusted man
" Familiarize thee with our play that lifts
" Thus, and thus lowers again, leg, arm and foot !
—Ensuring due correctness in the nude.   41
Which done, is all done ?   Not a whit, ye know !
He,—to art's surface rising from her depth,—
If some flax-polled soft-bearded sire be found,
May simulate a Joseph, (happy chance !)—   45
Limneth exact each wrinkle of the brow,
Loseth no involution, cheek or chap,
Till lo, in black and white, the senior lives !
Is it a young and comely peasant-nurse
That poseth ? (be the phrase accorded me !)   50
Each feminine delight of florid lip,
Eyes brimming o'er and brow bowed down with love,
Marmoreal neck and bosom uberous,—
Glad on the paper in a trice they go
To help his notion of the Mother-maid :   55
Methinks I see it, chalk a little stumped !
Yea and her babe—that flexure of soft limbs,
That budding face imbued with dewy sleep,
Contribute each an excellence to Christ.
Nay, since he humbly lent companionship,   60
Even the poor ass, unpanniered and elate

Stands, perks an ear up, he a model too ;
While clouted shoon, staff, scrip and water-gourd,—
Aught may betoken travel, heat and haste,—
No jot nor tittle of these but in its turn   65
Ministers to perfection of the piece :
Till now, such piece before him, part by part,—
Such prelude ended,—pause our painter may,
Submit his fifty studies one by one,
And in some sort boast "I have served my lords." 70

But what ?   And hath he painted once this while ?
Or when ye cry " Produce the thing required,
" Show us our picture shall rejoice its niche,
" Thy Journey through the Desert done in oils ! "—
What, doth he fall to shuffling 'mid his sheets,   75
Fumbling for first this, then the other fact
Consigned to paper,—" studies," bear the term !—
And stretch a canvas, mix a pot of paste,
And fasten here a head and there a tail,
(The ass hath one, my Judges !) so dove-tail   80
Or, rather, ass-tail in, piece sorrily out—
By bits of reproduction of the life—
The picture, the expected Family?
I trow not ! do I miss with my conceit
The mark, my lords?—not so my lords were served !
Rather your artist turns abrupt from these,   86

And preferably buries him and broods
(Quite away from aught vulgar and extern)
On the inner spectrum, filtered through the eye,
His brain-deposit, bred of many a drop,   90
E pluribus unum: and the wiser he !
For in that brain,—their fancy sees at work,
Could my lords peep indulged,—results alone,
Not processes which nourish such results,
Would they discover and appreciate,—life   95
Fed by digestion, not raw food itself,
No gobbets but smooth comfortable chyme
Secreted from each snapped-up crudity,—
Less distinct, part by part, but in the whole
Truer to the subject,—the main central truth   100
And soul o' the picture, would my Judges spy,—
Not those mere fragmentary studied facts
Which answer to the outward frame and flesh—
Not this nose, not that eyebrow, the other fact
Of man's staff, woman's stole or infant's clout,   105
But lo, a spirit-birth conceived of flesh,
Truth rare and real, not transcripts, fact and false.
The studies—for his pupils and himself !
The picture be for our eximious Rome
And—who, knows ?—satisfy its Governor,   110
Whose new wing to the villa he hath bought
(God give him joy of it) by Capena, soon

('T is bruited) shall be glowing with the brush
Of who hath long surpassed the Florentine,
The Urbinate and . . . what if I dared add,   115
Even his master, yea the Cortonese,—
I mean the accomplished Ciro Ferri, Sirs !
(—Did not he die ?   I 'll see before I print.)

End we exordium, Phœbus plucks my ear !
Thus then, just so and no whit otherwise,   120
Have I,—engaged as I were Ciro's self,
To paint a parallel, a Family,
The patriarch Pietro with his wise old wife
To boot (as if one introduced Saint Anne
By bold conjecture to complete the group)   125
And juvenile Pompilia with her babe,
Who, seeking safety in the wilderness,
Were all surprised by Herod, while outstretched
In sleep beneath a palm-tree by a spring,
And killed—the very circumstance I paint,   130
Moving the pity and terror of my lords—
Exactly so have I, a month at least,
Your Fiscal, made me cognizant of facts,
Searched out, pried into, pressed the meaning forth
Of every piece of evidence in point,   135
How bloody Herod slew these innocents,—
Until the glad result is gained, the group

Demonstrably presented in detail,
Their slumber and his onslaught,—like as life.
Yea and, availing me of help allowed   140
By law, discreet provision lest my lords
Be too much troubled by effrontery,—
The rack, law plies suspected crime withal—
(Law that hath listened while the lyrist sang
" *Lene tormentum ingenio admoves,*"   145
Gently thou joggest by a twinge the wit,
" *Plerumque duro,*" else were slow to blab !)
Through this concession my full cup runs o'er :
The guilty owns his guilt without reserve.
Therefore by part and part I clutch my case   150
Which, in entirety now,—momentous task,—
My lords demand, so render them I must,
Since, one poor pleading more and I have done.
But shall I ply my papers, play my proofs,
Parade my studies, fifty in a row,   155
As though the Court were yet in pupilage,
Claimed not the artist's ultimate appeal ?
Much rather let me soar the height prescribed
And, bowing low, proffer my picture's self !
No more of proof, disproof,—such virtue was, 160
Such vice was never in Pompilia, now !
Far better say " Behold Pompilia ! "—(for
I leave the family as unmanageable,

And stick to just one portrait, but life-size.)
Hath calumny imputed to the fair   165
A blemish, mole on cheek or wart on chin,
Much more, blind hidden horrors best unnamed?
Shall I descend to prove you, point by point,
Never was knock-knee known nor splay-foot found
In Phryne? (I must let the portrait go,   170
Content me with the model, I believe)—
—I prove this? An indignant sweep of hand,
Dash at and doing away with drapery,
And,—use your eyes, Athenians, smooth she smiles!
Or,—since my client can no longer smile,   175
And more appropriate instances abound,—
What is this Tale of Tarquin, how the slave
Was caught by him, preferred to Collatine?
Thou, even from thy corpse-clothes virginal,
Look'st the lie dead, Lucretia!   180
                              Thus at least
I, by the guidance of antiquity,
(Our one infallible guide) now operate,
Sure that the innocence thus shown is safe;
Sure, too, that, while I plead, the echoes cry   185
(Lend my weak voice thy trump, sonorous Fame!)
" Monstrosity the Phrynean shape shall mar,
" Lucretia's soul comport with Tarquin's lie,

" When thistles grow on vines or thorns yield figs,
" Or oblique sentence leave this judgment-seat ! " 190

A great theme : may my strength be adequate !
For—paint Pompilia, dares my feebleness?
How did I unaware engage so much
—Find myself undertaking to produce
A faultless nature in a flawless form?   195
What's here ?   Oh, turn aside nor dare the blaze
Of such a crown, such constellation, say,
As jewels here thy front, Humanity !
First, infancy, pellucid as a pearl ;
Then childhood—stone which, dew-drop at the'first,
(An old conjecture) sucks, by dint of gaze,   201
Blue from the sky and turns to sapphire so :
Yet both these gems eclipsed by, last and best,
Womanliness and wifehood opaline,
Its milk-white pallor,—chastity,—suffused   205
With here and there a tint and hint of flame,—
Desire,—the lapidary loves to find.
Such jewels bind conspicuously thy brow,
Pompilia, infant, child, maid, woman, wife—
Crown the ideal in our earth at last !   210
What should a faculty like mine do here?
Close eyes, or else, the rashlier hurry hand !

Which is to say,—lose no time but begin!
Sermocinando ne declamem, Sirs,
Ultra clepsydram, as our preachers smile,   215
Lest I exceed my hour-glass.   Whereupon,
As Flaccus prompts, I dare the epic plunge—
Begin at once with marriage, up till when
Little or nothing would arrest your love,
In the easeful life o' the lady ; lamb and lamb,   220
How do they differ?   Know one, you know all
Manners of maidenhood : mere maiden she.
And since all lambs are like in more than fleece,
Prepare to find that, lamb-like, she too frisks—
O' the weaker sex, my lords, the weaker sex !   225
To whom, the Teian teaches us, for gift,
Not strength,—man's dower,—but beauty, nature gave,
" Beauty in lieu of spears, in lieu of shields ! "
And what is beauty's sure concomitant,
Nay, intimate essential character,   230
But melting wiles, deliciousest deceits,
The whole redoubted armoury of love?
Therefore of vernal pranks, dishevellings
O' the hair of youth that dances April in,
And easily-imagined Hebe-slips   235
O'er sward which May makes over-smooth for foot—
These shall we pry into?—or wiselier wink,
Though numerous and dear they may have been?

For lo, advancing Hymen and his pomp!
Discedunt nunc amores, loves, farewell!   240
Maneat amor, let love, the sole, remain!
Farewell to dewiness and prime of life!
Remains the rough determined day : dance done,
To work, with plough and harrow!   What comes next?
'T is Guido henceforth guides Pompilia's step,   245
Cries "No more friskings o'er the foodful glebe,
"Else, 'ware the whip!"   Accordingly,—first crack
O' the thong,—we hear that his young wife was barred,
Cohibita fuit, from the old free life,
Vitam liberiorem ducere.   250
Demur we?   Nowise : heifer brave the hind?
We seek not there should lapse the natural law,
The proper piety to lord and king
And husband : let the heifer bear the yoke!
Only, I crave he cast not patience off,   255
This hind; for deem you she endures the whip,
Nor winces at the goad, nay, restive, kicks?
What if the adversary's charge be just,
And all untowardly she pursue her way
With groan and grunt, though hind strike ne'er so hard?
If petulant remonstrance made appeal,   261
Unseasonable, o'erprotracted,—if
Importunate challenge taxed the public ear
When silence more decorously had served

For protestation,—if Pompilian plaint   265
Wrought but to aggravate Guidonian ire,—
Why, such mishaps, ungainly though they be,
Ever companion change, are incident
To altered modes and novelty of life :
The philosophic mind expects no less,   270
Smilingly knows and names the crisis, sits
Waiting till old things go and new arrive.
Therefore, I hold a husband but inept
Who turns impatient at such transit-time,
As if this running from the rod would last!   275

Since, even while I speak, the end is reached :
Success awaits the soon-disheartened man.
The parents turn their backs and leave the house,
The wife may wail but none shall intervene :
He hath attained his object, groom and bride   280
Partake the nuptial bower no soul can see,
Old things are passed and all again is new,
Over and gone the obstacles to peace,
Novorum—tenderly the Mantuan turns
The expression, some such purpose in his eye—   285
Nascitur ordo ! Every storm is laid,
And forth from plain each pleasant herb may peep,
Each bloom of wifehood in abeyance late :
(Confer a passage in the Canticles.)

But what if, as 't is wont with plant and wife,   290
Flowers,—after a suppression to good end,
Still, when they do spring forth,—sprout here, spread
   there,
Anywhere likelier than beneath the foot
O' the lawful good-man gardener of the ground?
He dug and dibbled, sowed and watered,—still   295
'T is a chance wayfarer shall pluck the increase.
Just so, respecting persons not too much,
The lady, foes allege, put forth each charm
And proper floweret of feminity
To whosoever had a nose to smell   300
Or breast to deck : what if the charge be true?
The fault were graver had she looked with choice,
Fastidiously appointed who should grasp,
Who, in the whole town, go without the prize !
To nobody she destined donative,   305
But, first come was first served, the accuser saith.
Put case her sort of . . . in this kind . . . escapes
Were many and oft and indiscriminate—
Impute ye as the action were prepense,
The gift particular, arguing malice so?   310
Which butterfly of the wide air shall brag
" I was preferred to Guido "—when 't is clear
The cup, he quaffs at, lay with olent breast
Open to gnat, midge, bee and moth as well?

One chalice entertained the company;   315
And if its peevish lord object the more,
Mistake, misname such bounty in a wife,
Haste we to advertise him—charm of cheek,
Lustre of eye, allowance of the lip,
All womanly components in a spouse,   320
These are no household-bread each stranger's bite
Leaves by so much diminished for the mouth
O' the master of the house at supper-time :
But rather like a lump of spice they lie,
Morsel of myrrh, which scents the neighbourhood 325
Yet greets its lord no lighter by a grain.

Nay, even so, he shall be satisfied !
Concede we there was reason in his wrong,
Grant we his grievance and content the man !
For lo, Pompilia, she submits herself;   33c
Ere three revolving years have crowned their course,
Off and away she puts this same reproach
Of lavish bounty, inconsiderate gift
O' the sweets of wifehood stored to other ends :
No longer shall he blame "She none excludes,"   33!
But substitute " She laudably sees all,
" Searches the best out and selects the same."
For who is here, long sought and latest found,
Waiting his turn unmoved amid the whirl,

" *Constans in levitate,*"—Ha, my lords?　　　340
Calm in his levity,—indulge the quip !—
Since 't is a levite bears the bell away,
Parades him henceforth as Pompilia's choice.
'T is no ignoble object, husband !　Doubt'st?
When here comes tripping Flaccus with his phrase 345
" Trust me, no miscreant singled from the mob,
" *Crede non illum tibi de scelesta*
" *Plebe delectum,*" but a man of mark,
A priest, dost hear?　Why then, submit thyself !
Priest, ay and very phœnix of such fowl,　　350
Well-born, of culture, young and vigorous,
Comely too, since precise the precept points—
On the selected levite be there found
Nor mole nor scar nor blemish, lest the mind
Come all uncandid through the thwarting flesh !　355
Was not the son of Jesse ruddy, sleek,
Pleasant to look on, pleasant every way ?
Since well he smote the harp and sweetly sang,
And danced till Abigail came out to see,
And seeing smiled and smiling ministered　　360
The raisin-cluster and the cake of figs,
With ready meal refreshed the gifted youth,
Till Nabal, who was absent shearing sheep,
Felt heart sink, took to bed (discreetly done—
They might have been beforehand with him else) 365

And died—would Guido have behaved as well!
But ah, the faith of early days is gone,
Heu prisca fides!   Nothing died in him
Save courtesy, good sense and proper trust,
Which, when they ebb from souls they should o'erflow
Discover stub, weed, sludge and ugliness.   37
(The Pope, we know, is Neapolitan
And relishes a sea-side simile.)
Deserted by each charitable wave,
Guido, left high and dry, shows jealous now!   37.
Jealous avouched, paraded: tax the fool
With any peccadillo, he responds
" Truly I beat my wife through jealousy,
" Imprisoned her and punished otherwise,
" Being jealous: now would threaten, sword in hand,
" Now manage to mix poison in her sight,   38
" And so forth: jealously I dealt, in fine."
Concede thus much, and what remains to prove?
Have I to teach my masters what effect
Hath jealousy, and how, befooling men,   38
It makes false true, abuses eye and ear,
Turns mere mist adamantine, loads with sound
Silence, and into void and vacancy
Crowds a whole phalanx of conspiring foes?
Therefore who owns " I watched with jealousy   39
" My wife," adds " for no reason in the world!"

What need that, thus proved madman, he remark
" The thing I thought a serpent proved an eel "?—
Perchance the right Comacchian, six foot length,
And not an inch too long for that rare pie   395
(Master Arcangeli has heard of such)
Whose succulence makes fasting bearable;
Meant to regale some moody splenetic
Who, pleasing to mistake the donor's gift,
Spying I know not what Lernæan snake   400
I' the luscious Lenten creature, stamps forsooth
The dainty in the dust.

                  Enough! Prepare,
Such lunes announced, for downright lunacy!
Insanit homo, threat succeeds to threat,   405
And blow redoubles blow,—his wife, the block.
But, if a block, shall not she jar the hand
That buffets her? The injurious idle stone
Rebounds and hits the head of him who flung.
Causeless rage breeds, i' the wife now, rageful cause,
Tyranny wakes rebellion from its sleep.   411
Rebellion, say I?—rather, self-defence,
Laudable wish to live and see good days,
Pricks our Pompilia now to fly the fool
By any means, at any price,—nay, more,   415
Nay, most of all, i' the very interest

   X.   C

O' the fool that, baffled of his blind desire
At any price, were truliest victor so.
Shall he effect his crime and lose his soul ?
No, dictates duty to a loving wife !   420
Far better that the unconsummate blow,
Adroitly baulked by her, should back again,
Correctively admonish his own pate !

Crime then,—the Court is with me ?—she must crush :
How crush it ?   By all efficacious means ;   425
And these,—why, what in woman should they be ?
" With horns the bull, with teeth the lion fights ;
" To woman," quoth the lyrist quoted late,
" Nor teeth, nor horns, but beauty, Nature gave.
Pretty i' the Pagan !   Who dares blame the use   430
Of armoury thus allowed for natural,—
Exclaim against a seeming-dubious play
O' the sole permitted weapon, spear and shield
Alike, resorted to i' the circumstance
By poor Pompilia ?   Grant she somewhat plied   435
Arts that allure, the magic nod and wink,
The witchery of gesture, spell of word,
Whereby the likelier to enlist this friend,
Yea stranger, as a champion on her side ?
Such man, being but mere man, ('t was all she knew),
Must be made sure by beauty's silken bond,   441

The weakness that subdues the strong, and bows
Wisdom alike and folly. Grant the tale
O' the husband, which is false, were proved and true
To the letter—or the letters, I should say,   445
Abominations he professed to find
And fix upon Pompilia and the priest,—
Allow them hers—for though she could not write,
In early days of Eve-like innocence
That plucked no apple from the knowledge-tree, 450
Yet, at the Serpent's word, Eve plucks and eats
And knows—especially how to read and write :
And so Pompilia,—as the move o' the maw,
Quoth Persius, makes a parrot bid " Good day ! "
A crow salute the concave, and a pie   455
Endeavour at proficiency in speech,—
So she, through hunger after fellowship,
May well have learned, though late, to play the scribe :
As indeed, there 's one letter on the list
Explicitly declares did happen here.   460
" You thought my letters could be none of mine,"
She tells her parents—" mine, who wanted skill ;
" But now I have the skill, and write, you see ! "
She needed write love-letters, so she learned,
" *Negatas artifex sequi voces* "—though   465
This letter nowise 'scapes the common lot,
But lies i' the condemnation of the rest,

C 2

Found by the husband's self who forged them all.
Yet, for the sacredness of argument,
For this once an exemption shall it plead—   470
Anything, anything to let the wheels
Of argument run glibly to their goal!
Concede she wrote (which were preposterous)
This and the other epistle,—what of it?
Where does the figment touch her candid fame?   475
Being in peril of her life—"my life,
"Not an hour's purchase," as the letter runs,—
And having but one stay in this extreme,
Out of the wide world but a single friend—
What could she other than resort to him,   480
And how with any hope resort but thus?
Shall modesty dare bid a stranger brave
Danger, disgrace, nay death in her behalf—
Think to entice the sternness of the steel
Yet spare love's loadstone moving manly mind?   485
—Most of all, when such mind is hampered so
By growth of circumstance athwart the life
O' the natural man, that decency forbids
He stoop and take the common privilege,
Say frank "I love," as all the vulgar do.   490
A man is wedded to philosophy,
Married to statesmanship; a man is old;
A man is fettered by the foolishness

He took for wisdom and talked ten years since ;
A man is, like our friend the Canon here,　　　495
A priest, and wicked if he break his vow :
Shall he dare love, who may be Pope one day?
Despite the coil of such encumbrance here,
Suppose this man could love, unhappily,
And would love, dared he only let love show !　　500
In case the woman of his love, speaks first,
From what embarrassment she sets him free !
" 'T is I who break reserve, begin appeal,
" Confess that, whether you love me or no,
" I love you ! "　What an ease to dignity,　　　505
What help of pride from the hard high-backed chair
Down to the carpet where the kittens bask,
All under the pretence of gratitude !

From all which, I deduce—the lady here
Was bound to proffer nothing short of love　　510
To the priest whose service was to save her.　What ?
Shall she propose him lucre, dust o' the mine,
Rubbish o' the rock, some diamond, muckworms prize,
Some pearl secreted by a sickly fish?
Scarcely !　She caters for a generous taste.　　515
'T is love shall beckon, beauty bid to breast,
Till all the Samson sink into the snare !
Because, permit the end—permit therewith

Means to the end !
How say you, good my lords?
I hope you heard my adversary ring   521
The changes on this precept : now, let me
Reverse the peal !   *Quia dato licito fine,*
Ad illum assequendum ordinata
Non sunt damnanda media,—licit end   525
Enough was found in mere escape from death,
To legalize our means illicit else
Of feigned love, false allurement, fancied fact.
Thus Venus losing Cupid on a day,
(See that *Idyllium Moschi*) seeking help,   530
In the anxiety of motherhood,
Allowably promised " Who shall bring report
" Where he is wandered to, my winged babe,
" I give him for reward a nectared kiss ;
" But who brings safely back the truant's self,   535
" His be a super-sweet makes kiss seem cold ! "
Are not these things writ for example-sake ?

To such permitted motive, then, refer
All those professions, else were hard explain,
Of hope, fear, jealousy, and the rest of love !   540
He is Myrtillus, Amaryllis she,
She burns, he freezes,—all a mere device
To catch and keep the man, may save her life,

Whom otherwise nor catches she nor keeps!
Worst, once, turns best now: in all faith, she feigns:
Feigning,—the liker innocence to guilt,   546
The truer to the life in what she feigns!
How if Ulysses,—when, for public good
He sunk particular qualms and played the spy,
Entered Troy's hostile gate in beggar's garb—   550
How if he first had boggled at this clout,
Grown dainty o'er that clack-dish? Grime is grace
To whoso gropes amid the dung for gold.

Hence, beyond promises, we praise each proof
That promise was not simply made to break,   555
Mere moonshine-structure meant to fade at dawn:
We praise, as consequent and requisite,
What, enemies allege, were more than words,
Deeds—meetings at the window, twilight-trysts,
Nocturnal entertainments in the dim   560
Old labyrinthine palace; lies, we know—
Inventions we, long since, turned inside out.
Must such external semblance of intrigue
Demonstrate that intrigue there lurks perdue?
Does every hazel-sheath disclose a nut?   565
He were a Molinist who dared maintain
That midnight meetings in a screened alcove
Must argue folly in a matron—since

So would he bring a slur on Judith's self,
Commended beyond women, that she lured   570
The lustful to destruction through his lust.
Pompilia took not Judith's liberty, .
No faulchion find you in her hand to smite,
No damsel to convey in dish the head
Of Holophernes,—style the Canon so—   575
Or is it the Count? If I entangle me
With my similitudes,—if wax wings melt,
And earthward down I drop, not mine the fault :
Blame your beneficence, O Court, O sun,
Whereof the beamy smile affects my flight !   580
What matter, so Pompilia's fame revive
I' the warmth that proves the bane of Icarus?

Yea, we have shown it lawful, necessary
Pompilia leave her husband, seek the house
O' the parents : and because 'twixt home and home
Lies a long road with many a danger rife,   586
Lions by the way and serpents in the path,
To rob and ravish,—much behoves she keep
Each shadow of suspicion from fair fame,
For her own sake much, but for his sake more,   590
The ingrate husband's.   Evidence shall be,
Plain witness to the world how white she walks
I' the mire she wanders through ere Rome she reach.

And who so proper witness as a priest?
Gainsay ye? Let me hear who dares gainsay! 595
I hope we still can punish heretics!
'"Give me the man" I say with him of Gath,
"That we may fight together!" None, I think:
The priest is granted me.

           Then, if a priest, 600
One juvenile and potent: else, mayhap,
That dragon, our Saint George would slay, slays
    him.
And should fair face accompany strong hand,
The more complete equipment: nothing mars
Work, else praiseworthy, like a bodily flaw 605
I' the worker: as 't is said Saint Paul himself
Deplored the check o' the puny presence, still
Cheating his fulmination of its flash,
Albeit the bolt therein went true to oak.
Therefore the agent, as prescribed, she takes,— 610
Both juvenile and potent, handsome too,—
In all obedience: "good," you grant again.
Do you? I would you were the husband, lords!
How prompt and facile might departure be!
How boldly would Pompilia and the priest 615
March out of door, spread flag at beat of drum,
But that inapprehensive Guido grants

Neither premiss nor yet conclusion here,
And, purblind, dreads a bear in every bush !
For his own quietude and comfort, then,   620
Means must be found for flight in masquerade
At hour when all things sleep.—" Save jealousy ! "
Right, Judges !   Therefore shall the lady's wit
Supply the boon thwart nature baulks him of,
And do him service with the potent drug   625
(Helen's nepenthe, as my lords opine) .
Which respites blessedly each fretted nerve
O' the much-enduring man : accordingly,
There lies he, duly dosed and sound asleep,
Relieved of woes or real or raved about.   630
While soft she leaves his side, he shall not wake ;
Nor stop who steals away to join her friend,
Nor do him mischief should he catch that friend
Intent on more than friendly office,—nay,
Nor get himself raw head and bones laid bare   635
In payment of his apparition !

                              Thus
Would I defend the step,—were the thing true
Which is a fable,—see my former speech,—
That Guido slept (who never slept a wink)   640
Through treachery, an opiate from his wife,
Who not so much as knew what opiates mean.

Now she may start: or hist,—a stoppage still !
A journey is an enterprise of cost !
As in campaigns, we fight but others pay,   645
Suis expensis, nemo militat.
'T is Guido's self we guard from accident,
Ensuring safety to Pompilia, versed
Nowise in misadventures by the way,
Hard riding and rough quarters, the rude fare,   650
The unready host.   What magic mitigates
Each plague of travel to the unpractised wife ?
Money, sweet Sirs !   And were the fiction fact
She helped herself thereto with liberal hand
From out her husband's store,—what fitter use   655
Was ever husband's money destined to ?
With bag and baggage thus did Dido once
Decamp,—for more authority, a queen !

So is she fairly on her route at last,
Prepared for either fortune : nay and if   660
The priest, now all a-glow with enterprise,
Cool somewhat presently when fades the flush
O' the first adventure, clouded o'er belike
By doubts, misgivings how the day may die,
Though born with such auroral brilliance,—if   665
The brow seem over-pensive and the lip ·
'Gin lag and lose the prattle lightsome late,—

Vanquished by tedium of a prolonged jaunt
In a close carriage o'er a jolting road,
With only one young female substitute   670
For seventeen other Canons of ripe age
Were wont to keep him company in church,—
Shall not Pompilia haste to dissipate
The silent cloud that, gathering, bodes her bale ?—
Prop the irresoluteness may portend   675
Suspension of the project, check the flight,
Bring ruin on them both ?   Use every means,
Since means to the end are lawful !   What i' the way
Of wile should have allowance like a kiss
Sagely and sisterly administered,   680
Sororia saltem oscula?   We find
Such was the remedy her wit applied
To each incipient scruple of the priest,
If we believe,—as, while my wit is mine
I cannot,—what the driver testifies,   685
Borsi, called Venerino, the mere tool
Of Guido and his friend the Governor,—
Avowal I proved wrung from out the wretch,
After long rotting in imprisonment,
As price of liberty and favour : long   690
They tempted, he at last succumbed, and lo
Counted them out full tale each kiss and more,
" The journey being one long embrace," quoth he.

Still, though we should believe the driver's lie,
Nor even admit as probable excuse,   695
Right reading of the riddle,—as I urged
In my first argument, with fruit perhaps—
That what the owl-like eyes (at back of head!)
O' the driver, drowsed by driving night and day,
Supposed a vulgar interchange of lips,   700
This was but innocent jog of head 'gainst head,
Cheek meeting jowl as apple may touch pear
From branch and branch contiguous in the wind,
When Autumn blusters and the orchard rocks :—
That rapid run and the rough road were cause   705
O' the casual ambiguity, no harm
I' the world to eyes awake and penetrative.
Say,—not to grasp a truth I can release
And safely fight without, yet conquer still,—
Say, she kissed him, say, he kissed her again!   710
Such osculation was a potent means,
A very efficacious help, no doubt:
Such with a third part of her nectar did
Venus imbue: why should Pompilia fling
The poet's declaration in his teeth?—   715
Pause to employ what —since it had success,
And kept the priest her servant to the end—
We must presume of energy enough,
No whit superfluous, so permissible?

The goal is gained: day, night and yet a day   720
Have run their round : a long and devious road
Is traversed,—many manners, various men
Passed in review, what cities did they see,
What hamlets mark, what profitable food
For after-meditation cull and store !   725
Till Rome, that Rome whereof—this voice
Would it might make our Molinists observe,
That she is built upon a rock nor shall
Their powers prevail against her !—Rome, I say,
Is all but reached ; one stage more and they stop 730
Saved : pluck up heart, ye pair, and forward, then !

Ah, Nature—baffled she recurs, alas !
Nature imperiously exacts her due,
Spirit is willing but the flesh is weak :
Pompilia needs must acquiesce and swoon,   735
Give hopes alike and fears a breathing-while.
The innocent sleep soundly : sound she sleeps,
So let her slumber, then, unguarded save
By her own chastity, a triple mail,
And his good hand whose stalwart arms have borne 740
The sweet and senseless burthen like a babe
From coach to couch,—the serviceable strength !
Nay, what and if he gazed rewardedly
On the pale beauty prisoned in embrace,

Stooped over, stole a balmy breath perhaps   745
For more assurance sleep was not decease—
" *Ut vidi*," "how I saw!" succeeded by
" *Ut perii*," "how I sudden lost my brains!"
—What harm ensued to her unconscious quite?
For, curiosity—how natural!   750
Importunateness—what a privilege
In the ardent sex! And why curb ardour here?
How can the priest but pity whom he saved?
And pity is so near to love, and love
So neighbourly to all unreasonableness!   755
As to love's object, whether love were sage
Or foolish, could Pompilia know or care,
Being still sound asleep, as I premised?
Thus the philosopher absorbed by thought,
Even Archimedes, busy o'er a book   760
The while besiegers sacked his Syracuse,
Was ignorant of the imminence o' the point
O' the sword till it surprised him : let it stab,
And never knew himself was dead at all.
So sleep thou on, secure whate'er betide !   765
For thou, too, hast thy problem hard to solve—
How so much beauty is compatible
With so much innocence !

                          Fit place, methinks,

While in this task she rosily is lost,   770
To treat of and repel objection here
Which,—frivolous, I grant,—my mind misgives,
May somehow still have flitted, gadfly-like,
And teased the Court at times—as if, all said
And done, there seemed, the Court might nearly say,
In a certain acceptation, somewhat more   776
Of what may pass for insincerity,
Falsehood, throughout the course Pompilia took,
Than befits Christian.   Pagans held, we know,
Man always ought to aim at good and truth,   780
Not always put one thing in the same words :
Non idem semper dicere sed spectare
Debemus.   But the Pagan yoke was light ;
" Lie not at all," the exacter precept bids :
Each least lie breaks the law,—is sin, we hold.   785
I humble me, but venture to submit—
What prevents sin, itself is sinless, sure :
And sin, which hinders sin of deeper dye,
Softens itself away by contrast so.
Conceive me !   Little sin, by none at all,   790
Were properly condemned for great : but great,
By greater, dwindles into small again.
Now, what is greatest sin of womanhood?
That which unwomans it, abolishes
The nature of the woman,—impudence.   795

Who contradicts me here? Concede me, then,
Whatever friendly fault may interpose
To save the sex from self-abolishment
Is three-parts on the way to virtue's rank !
And, what is taxed here as duplicity,   800
Feint, wile and trick,—admitted for the nonce,—
What worse do one and all than interpose,
Hold, as it were, a deprecating hand,
Statuesquely, in the Medicean mode,
Before some shame which modesty would veil?   805
Who blames the gesture prettily perverse?
Thus,—lest ye miss a point illustrative,—
Admit the husband's calumny—allow
That the wife, having penned the epistle fraught
With horrors, charge on charge of crime she heaped
O' the head of Pietro and Violante—(still   811
Presumed her parents)—having despatched the same
To their arch-enemy Paolo, through free choice
And no sort of compulsion in the world—
Put case she next discards simplicity   815
For craft, denies the voluntary act,
Declares herself a passive instrument
I' the husband's hands ; that, duped by knavery,
She traced the characters she could not write,
And took on trust the unread sense which, read,   820
And recognized were to be spurned at once :
    X.   D

Allow this calumny, I reiterate !
Who is so dull as wonder at the pose
Of our Pompilia in the circumstance?
Who sees not that the too-ingenuous soul,   825
Repugnant even at a duty done
Which brought beneath too scrutinizing glare
The misdemeanours,—buried in the dark,—
Of the authors of her being, as believed,—
Stung to the quick at her impulsive deed,   830
And willing to repair what harm it worked,
She—wise in this beyond what Nero proved,
Who when folk urged the candid juvenile
To sign the warrant, doom the guilty dead,
" Would I had never learned to write," quoth he !
—Pompilia rose above the Roman, cried   836
" To read or write I never learned at all ! "
O splendidly mendacious !

                              But time fleets:
Let us not linger: hurry to the end,   840
Since flight does end, and that disastrously.
Beware ye blame desert for unsuccess,
Disparage each expedient else to praise,
Call failure folly !   Man's best effort fails.
After ten years' resistance Troy succumbed :   845
Could valour save a town, Troy still had stood.

Pompilia came off halting in no point
Of courage, conduct, her long journey through :
But nature sank exhausted at the close,
And as I said, she swooned and slept all night.   850
Morn breaks and brings the husband : we assist
At the spectacle.   Discovery succeeds.
Ha, how is this?   What moonstruck rage is here?
Though we confess to partial frailty now,
To error in a woman and a wife,   855
Is 't by the rough way she shall be reclaimed?
Who bursts upon her chambered privacy?
What crowd profanes the chaste *cubiculum ?*
What outcries and lewd laughter, scurril gibe
And ribald jest to scare the ministrant   860
Good angels that commerce with souls in sleep?
Why, had the worst crowned Guido to his wish,
Confirmed his most irrational surmise,
Yet there be bounds to man's emotion, checks
To an immoderate astonishment.   865
'T is decent horror, regulated wrath,
Befit our dispensation : have we back
The old Pagan license?   Shall a Vulcan clap
His net o' the sudden and expose the pair
To the unquenchable universal mirth?   870
A feat, antiquity saw scandal in ·
So clearly, that the nauseous tale thereof—

D 2

Demodocus his nugatory song—
Hath ever been concluded modern stuff
Impossible to the mouth of the grave Muse,   875
So, foisted into that Eighth Odyssey
By some impertinent pickthank. O thou fool,
Count Guido Franceschini, what didst gain
By publishing thy secret to the world?
Were all the precepts of the wise a waste—   880
Bred in thee not one touch of reverence?
Admit thy wife—admonish we the fool,—
Were falseness' self, why chronicle thy shame?
Much rather should thy teeth bite out thy tongue,
Dumb lip consort with desecrated brow,   885
Silence become historiographer,
And thou—thine own Cornelius Tacitus!
But virtue, barred, still leaps the barrier, lords!
—Still, moon-like, penetrates the encroaching mist
And bursts, all broad and bare, on night, ye know!
Surprised, then, in the garb of truth, perhaps,   891
Pompilia, thus opposed, breaks obstacle,
Springs to her feet, and stands Thalassian-pure,
Confronts the foe,—nay, catches at his sword
And tries to kill the intruder, he complains.   895
Why, so she gave her lord his lesson back,
Crowned him, this time, the virtuous woman's way,
With an exact obedience; he brought sword,

She drew the same, since swords are meant to draw.
Tell not me 't is sharp play with tools on edge!   900
It was the husband chose the weapon here.
Why did not he inaugurate the game
With some gentility of apophthegm
Still pregnant on the philosophic page,
Some captivating cadence still a-lisp   905
O' the poet's lyre?   Such spells subdue the surge,
Make tame the tempest, much more mitigate
The passions of the mind, and probably
Had moved Pompilia to a smiling blush.
No, he must needs prefer the argument   910
O' the blow: and she obeyed, in duty bound,
Returned him buffet ratiocinative—
Ay, in the reasoner's own interest,
For wife must follow whither husband leads,
Vindicate honour as himself prescribes,   915
Save him the very way himself bids save!
No question but who jumps into a quag
Should stretch forth hand and pray us "Pull me
          out
" By the hand!" such were the customary cry:
But Guido pleased to bid "Leave hand alone!   920
" Join both feet, rather, jump upon my head:
" I extricate myself by the rebound!"
And dutifully as enjoined she jumped—

Drew his own sword and menaced his own life,
Anything to content a wilful spouse.   925

And so he was contented—one must do
Justice to the expedient which succeeds,
Strange as it seem : at flourish of the blade,
The crowd drew back, stood breathless and abashed,
Then murmured "This should be no wanton wife,   930
" No conscience-stricken sinner, caught i' the act,
" And patiently awaiting our first stone :
" But a poor hard-pressed all-bewildered thing,
" Has rushed so far, misguidedly perhaps,
" Meaning no more harm than a frightened sheep.   935
" She sought for aid ; and if she made mistake
" I' the man could aid most, why—so mortals do :
" Even the blessed Magdalen mistook
" Far less forgiveably: consult the place—
" Supposing him to be the gardener,   940
" ' Sir,' said she, and so following."   Why more words?
Forthwith the wife is pronounced innocent :
What would the husband more than gain his cause,
And find that honour flash in the world's eye,
His apprehension was lest soil had smirched?   945

So, happily the adventure comes to close
Whereon my fat opponent grounds his charge

Preposterous : at mid-day he groans "How dark ! "
Listen to me, thou Archangelic swine !
Where is the ambiguity to blame,   950
The flaw to find in our Pompilia?   Safe
She stands, see !   Does thy comment follow quick
" Safe, inasmuch as at the end proposed ;
" But thither she picked way by devious path—
" Stands dirtied, no dubiety at all !   955
" I recognize success, yet, all the same,
" Importunately will suggestion prompt—
" Better Pompilia gained the right to boast
" ' No devious path, no doubtful patch was mine,
" ' I saved my head nor sacrificed my foot : '   960
" Why, being in a peril, show mistrust
" Of the angels set to guard the innocent?
" Why rather hold by obvious vulgar help
" Of stratagem and subterfuge, excused
" Somewhat, but still no less a foil, a fault,   965
" Since low with high, and good with bad is linked?
" Methinks I view some ancient bas-relief.
" There stands Hesione thrust out by Troy,
" Her father's hand has chained her to a crag,
" Her mother's from the virgin plucked the vest,   970
" At a safe distance both distressful watch,
" While near and nearer comes the snorting orc.
" I look that, white and perfect to the end,

" She wait till Jove despatch some demigod;
" Not that,—impatient of celestial club   975
" Alcmena's son should brandish at the beast,—
' She daub, disguise her dainty limbs with pitch,
" And so elude the purblind monster!   Ay,
" The trick succeeds, but 't is an ugly trick,
" Where needs have been no trick ! "   980

                         My answer?   Faugh;
Nimis incongrue!   Too absurdly put !
Sententiam ego teneo contrariam,
Trick, I maintain, had no alternative.
The heavens were bound with brass,—Jove far at feast
(No feast like that thou didst not ask me to,   986
Arcangeli,—I heard of thy regale !)
With the unblamed Æthiop,—Hercules spun wool
I' the lap of Omphale, while Virtue shrieked—
The brute came paddling all the faster.   You   990
Of Troy, who stood at distance, where 's the aid
You offered in the extremity?   Most and least,
Gentle and simple, here the Governor,
There the Archbishop, everywhere the friends,
Shook heads and waited for a miracle,   995
Or went their way, left Virtue to her fate.
Just this one rough and ready man leapt forth !
—Was found, sole anti-Fabius (dare I say)'

Who restored things, with no delay at all,
Qui haud cunctando rem restituit! He,   1000
He only, Caponsacchi 'mid a crowd,
Caught Virtue up, carried Pompilia off
Through gaping impotence of sympathy
In ranged Arezzo : what you take for pitch,
Is nothing worse, belike, than black and blue,   1005
Mere evanescent proof that hardy hands
Did yeoman's service, cared not where the gripe
Was more than duly energetic : bruised,
She smarts a little, but her bones are saved
A fracture, and her skin will soon show sleek.   1010
How it disgusts when weakness, false-refined,
Censures the honest rude effective strength,—
When sickly dreamers of the impossible
Decry plain sturdiness which does the feat
With eyes wide open !   1015
          Did occasion serve,
I could illustrate, if my lords allow ;
Quid vetat, what forbids I aptly ask
With Horace, that I give my anger vent,
While I let breathe, no less, and recreate,   1020
The gravity of my Judges, by a tale ?
A case in point—what though an apologue
Graced by tradition ?—possibly a fact :
Tradition must precede all scripture, words

Serve as our warrant ere our books can be :   1025
So, to tradition back we needs must go
For any fact's authority : and this
Hath lived so far (like jewel hid in muck)
On page of that old lying vanity
Called " Sepher Toldoth Yeschu : " God be praised,
I read no Hebrew,—take the thing on trust :   1031
But I believe the writer meant no good
(Blind as he was to truth in some respects)
To our pestiferous and schismatic . . . well,
My lords' conjecture be the touchstone, show   1035
The thing for what it is !   The author lacks
Discretion, and his zeal exceeds : but zeal,—
How rare in our degenerate day !   Enough !
Here is the story : fear not, I shall chop
And change a little, else my Jew would press   1040
All too unmannerly before the Court.

It happened once,—begins this foolish Jew,
Pretending to write Christian history,—
That three, held greatest, best and worst of men,
Peter and John and Judas, spent a day   1045
In toil and travel through the country-side
On some sufficient business—I suspect,
Suppression of some Molinism i' the bud.
Foot-sore and hungry, dropping with fatigue,

They reached by nightfall a poor lonely grange,   1050
Hostel or inn : so, knocked and entered there.
" Your pleasure, great ones ? "—" Shelter, rest and food ! "
For shelter, there was one bare room above ;
For rest therein, three beds of bundled straw :
For food, one wretched starveling fowl, no more—
Meat for one mouth, but mockery for three.   1056
" You have my utmost."   How should supper serve?
Peter broke silence : " To the spit with fowl !
" And while 't is cooking, sleep !—since beds there be,
" And, so far, satisfaction of a want.   1060
" Sleep we an hour, awake at supper-time,
" Then each of us narrate the dream he had,
" And he whose dream shall prove the happiest, point
" The clearliest out the dreamer as ordained
" Beyond his fellows to receive the fowl,   1065
" Him let our shares be cheerful tribute to,
" His the entire meal, may it do him good ! "
Who could dispute so plain a consequence?
So said, so done : each hurried to his straw,
Slept his hour's-sleep and dreamed his dream, and woke.
" I," commenced John, " dreamed that I gained the
         prize   1071
" We all aspire to : the proud place was mine,
" Throughout the earth and to the end of time
" I was the Loved Disciple : mine the meal ! "

" But I," proceeded Peter, "dreamed, a word   1075
" Gave me the headship of our company,
" Made me the Vicar and Vice-gerent, gave
" The keys of heaven and hell into my hand,
" And o'er the earth, dominion : mine the meal ! "
" While I," submitted in soft under-tone   1080
The Iscariot—sense of his unworthiness
Turning each eye up to the inmost white—
With long-drawn sigh, yet letting both lips smack,
" I have had just the pitifullest dream
" That ever proved man meanest of his mates,   1085
" And born foot-washer and foot-wiper, nay
" Foot-kisser to each comrade of you all !
" I dreamed I dreamed ; and in that mimic dream
" (Impalpable to dream as dream to fact)
" Methought I meanly chose to sleep no wink   1090
" But wait until I heard my brethren snore ;
" Then stole from couch, slipped noiseless o'er the
    planks,
" Slid downstairs, furtively approached the hearth,
  " Found the fowl duly brown, both back and breast,
" Hissing in harmony with the cricket's chirp,   1095
" Grilled to a point ; said no grace but fell to,
" Nor finished till the skeleton lay bare.
" In penitence for which ignoble dream,
" Lo, I renounce my portion cheerfully !

"Fie on the flesh—be mine the ethereal gust,   1100
" And yours the sublunary sustenance !
"See that whate'er be left ye give the poor ! "
Down the two scuttled, one on other's heel,
Stung by a fell surmise ; and found, alack,
A goodly savour, both the drumstick bones,   1105
And that which henceforth took the appropriate name
O' the Merry-thought, in memory of the fact
That to keep wide awake is man's best dream.

So,—as was said once of Thucydides
And his sole joke, " The lion, lo, hath laughed ! "—
Just so, the Governor and all that 's great   1111
I' the city, never meant that Innocence
Should quite starve while Authority sat at meat ;
They meant to fling a bone at banquet's end :
Wished well to our Pompilia—in their dreams,   1115
Nor bore the secular sword in vain—asleep.
Just so the Archbishop and all good like him
Went to bed meaning to pour oil and wine
I' the wounds of her, next day,—but long ere day,
They had burned the one and drunk the other, while
Just so, again, contrariwise, the priest   1121
Sustained poor Nature in extremity
By stuffing barley-bread into her mouth,
Saving Pompilia (grant the parallel)

By the plain homely and straightforward way   1125
Taught him by common sense.   Let others shriek
"Oh what refined expedients did we dream
"Proved us the only fit to help the fair ! "
He cried "A carriage waits, jump in with me ! "

And now, this application pardoned, lords,—   1130
This recreative pause and breathing-while,—
Back to beseemingness and gravity !
For Law steps in : Guido appeals to Law,
Demands she arbitrate,—does well for once.
O Law, of thee how neatly was it said   1135
By that old Sophocles, thou hast thy seat
I' the very breast of Jove, no meanlier throned !
Here is a piece of work now, hitherto
Begun and carried on, concluded near,
Without an eye-glance cast thy sceptre's way ;   1140
And, lo the stumbling and discomfiture !
Well may you call them "lawless" means, men take
To extricate themselves through mother-wit
When tangled haply in the toils of life !
Guido would try conclusions with his foe,   1145
Whoe'er the foe was and whate'er the offence ;
He would recover certain dowry-dues :
Instead of asking Law to lend a hand,
What pother of sword drawn and pistol cocked,

What peddling with forged letters and paid spies,
Politic circumvention!—all to end 1151
As it began—by loss of the fool's head,
First in a figure, presently in a fact.
It is a lesson to mankind at large.
How other were the end, would men be sage 1155
And bear confidingly each quarrel straight,
O Law, to thy recipient mother-knees !
How would the children light come and prompt go,
This with a red-cheeked apple for reward,
The other, peradventure red-cheeked too 1160
I' the rear, by taste of birch for punishment.
No foolish brawling murder any more !
Peace for the household, practise for the Fisc,
And plenty for the exchequer of my lords !
Too much to hope, in this world : in the next, 1165
Who knows ? Since, why should sit the Twelve enthroned
To judge the tribes, unless the tribes be judged ?
And 't is impossible but offences come :
So, all 's one lawsuit, all one long leet-day !

Forgive me this digression—that I stand 1170
Entranced awhile at Law's first beam, outbreak
O' the business, when the Count's good angel bade
" Put up thy sword, born enemy to the ear,
" And let Law listen to thy difference ! "

And Law does listen and compose the strife,   1175
Settle the suit, how wisely and how well!
On our Pompilia, faultless to a fault,
Law bends a brow maternally severe,
Implies the worth of perfect chastity,
By fancying the flaw she cannot find.   1180
Superfluous sifting snow, nor helps nor harms:
'T is safe to censure levity in youth,
Tax womanhood with indiscretion, sure!
Since toys, permissible to-day, become
Follies to-morrow: prattle shocks in church: 1185
And that curt skirt which lets a maiden skip,
The matron changes for a trailing robe.
Mothers may aim a blow with half-shut eyes
Nodding above their spindles by the fire,
And chance to hit some hidden fault, else safe.   1190
Just so, Law hazarded a punishment—
If applicable to the circumstance,
Why, well! if not so apposite, well too.
" Quit the gay range o' the world," I hear her cry,
" Enter, in lieu, the penitential pound :   1195
" Exchange the gauds of pomp for ashes, dust !
" Leave each mollitious haunt of luxury !
" The golden-garnished silken-couched alcove,
" The many-columned terrace that so tempts
" Feminine soul put foot forth, extend ear·   1200

"To fluttering joy of lover's serenade,—
"Leave these for cellular seclusion ! mask
"And dance no more, but fast and pray ! avaunt—
"Be burned, thy wicked townsman's sonnet-book !
"Welcome, mild hymnal by . . . some better scribe !
"For the warm arms were wont enfold thy flesh, 1206
"Let wire-shirt plough and whipcord discipline ! "
If such an exhortation proved, perchance,
Inapplicable, words bestowed in waste,
What harm, since Law has store, can spend nor miss ?

And so, our paragon submits herself,   1211
Goes at command into the holy house,
And, also at command, comes out again :
For, could the effect of such obedience prove
Too certain, too immediate ?   Being healed,   1215
Go blaze abroad the matter, blessed one !
Art thou sound forthwith ?   Speedily vacate
The step by pool-side, leave Bethesda free
To patients plentifully posted round,
Since the whole need not the physician !   Brief, 1220
She may betake her to her parents' place.
Welcome her, father, with wide arms once more,
Motion her, mother, to thy breast again !
For why ?   Since Law relinquishes the charge,
Grants to your dwelling-place a prison's style,   1225

X.   E

Rejoice you with Pompilia ! golden days,
Redeunt Saturnia regna.   Six weeks slip,
And she is domiciled in house and home
As though she thence had never budged at all.
And thither let the husband,—joyous, ay,   1230
But contrite also—quick betake himself,
Proud that his dove which lay among the pots
Hath mued those dingy feathers,—moulted now,
Shows silver bosom clothed with yellow gold !
So shall he tempt her to the perch she fled,   1235
Bid to domestic bliss the truant back.

But let him not delay !   Time fleets how fast,
And opportunity, the irrevocable,
Once flown will flout him !   Is the furrow traced ?
If field with corn ye fail preoccupy,   1240
Darnel for wheat and thistle-beards for grain,
Infelix lolium, carduus horridus,
Will grow apace in combination prompt,
Defraud the husbandman of his desire.
Already—hist—what murmurs 'monish now   1245
The laggard ?—doubtful, nay, fantastic bruit
Of such an apparition, such return
Interdum, to anticipate the spouse,
Of Caponsacchi's very self !   'T is said,
When nights are lone and company is rare,   1250

His visitations brighten winter up.
If so they did—which nowise I believe—
(How can I?—proof abounding that the priest,
Once fairly at his relegation-place,
Never once left it) still, admit he stole   1255
A midnight march, would fain see friend again,
Find matter for instruction in the past,
Renew the old adventure in such chat
As cheers a fireside! He was lonely too,
He, too, must need his recreative hour.   '   1260
Shall it amaze the philosophic mind
If he, long wont the empurpled cup to quaff,
Have feminine society at will,
Being debarred abruptly from all drink
Save at the spring which Adam used for wine,   1265
Dreads harm to just the health he hoped to guard,
And, trying abstinence, gains malady?
Ask Tozzi, now physician to the Pope!
"Little by little break"—(I hear he bids
Master Arcangeli my antagonist,   1270
Who loves good cheer, and may indulge too much:
So I explain the logic of the plea
Wherewith he opened our proceedings late)—
"Little by little break a habit, Don,
"Become necessity to feeble flesh!"   1275
And thus, nocturnal taste of intercourse

(Which never happened,—but, suppose it did)
May have been used to dishabituate
By sip and sip this drainer to the dregs
O' the draught of conversation,—heady stuff,   1280
Brewage which, broached, it took two days and nights
To properly discuss i' the journey, Sirs !
Such power has second-nature, men call use,
That undelightful objects get to charm
Instead of chafe : the daily colocynth   1285
Tickles the palate by repeated dose,
Old sores scratch kindly, the ass makes a push,
Although the mill-yoke-wound be smarting yet,
For mill-door bolted on a holiday :
Nor must we marvel here if impulse urge   1290
To talk the old story over now and then,
The hopes and fears, the stoppage and the haste,—
Subjects of colloquy to surfeit once.
" Here did you bid me twine a rosy wreath ! "
" And there you paid my lips a compliment ! "   1295
" Here you admired the tower could be so tall ! "
" And there you likened that of Lebanon
" To the nose of the beloved ! "   Trifles ! still,
" *Forsan et hæc olim*,"—such trifles serve
To make the minutes pass in winter-time.   1300

Husband, return then, I re-counsel thee !

For, finally, of all glad circumstance
Should make a prompt return imperative,
What in the world awaits thee, dost suppose?
O' the sudden, as good gifts are wont befall,　　1305
What is the hap of our unconscious Count?
That which lights bonfire and sets cask a-tilt,
Dissolves the stubborn'st heart in jollity.
O admirable, there is born a babe,
A son, an heir, a Franceschini last　　1310
And best o' the stock! Pompilia, thine the palm!
Repaying incredulity with faith,
Ungenerous thrift of each marital debt
With bounty in profuse expenditure,
Pompilia scorns to have the old year end　　1315
Without a present shall ring in the new—
Bestows on her too-parsimonious lord
An infant for the apple of his eye,
Core of his heart, and crown completing life,
True *summum bonum* of the earthly lot!　　1320
" We," saith ingeniously the sage, " are born
" Solely that others may be born of us."
So, father, take thy child, for thine that child,
Oh nothing doubt! In wedlock born, law holds
Baseness impossible: since "*filius est*　　1325
" *Quem nuptiæ demonstrant*," twits the text
Whoever dares to doubt.

Yet doubt he dares!
O faith, where art thou flown from out the world?
Already on what an age of doubt we fall!   1330
Instead of each disputing for the prize,
The babe is bandied here from that to this.
Whose the babe?   " *Cujum pecus?* " Guido's lamb?
" *An Melibœi?* "   Nay, but of the priest!
" *Non sed Ægonis!* "   Someone must be sire: 1335
And who shall say, in such a puzzling strait,
If there were not vouchsafed some miracle
To the wife who had been harassed and abused
More than enough by Guido's family
For non-production of the promised fruit   1340
Of marriage?   What if Nature, I demand,
Touched to the quick by taunts upon her sloth,
Had roused herself, put forth recondite power,
Bestowed this birth to vindicate her sway,
Like the strange favour, Maro memorized   1345
As granted Aristæus when his hive
Lay empty of the swarm? not one more bee—
Not one more babe to Franceschini's house!
And lo, a new birth filled the air with joy,
Sprung from the bowels of the generous steer,   1350
A novel son and heir rejoiced the Count!
Spontaneous generation, need I prove
Were facile feat to Nature at a pinch?

Let whoso doubts, steep horsehair certain weeks
In water, there will be produced a snake ;   1355
Spontaneous product of the horse, which horse
Happens to be the representative—
Now that I think on 't—of Arezzo's self,
The very city our conception blessed :
Is not a prancing horse the City-arms ?   1360
What sane eye fails to see coincidence ?
Cur ego, boast thou, my Pompilia, then,
Desperem fieri sine conjuge
Mater—how well the Ovidian distich suits !—
Et parere intacto dummodo   1365
Casta viro ? Such miracle was wrought !
Note, further, as to mark the prodigy,
The babe in question neither took the name
Of Guido, from the sire presumptive, nor
Giuseppe, from the sire potential, but   1370
Gaetano—last saint of our hierarchy,
And newest namer for a thing so new !
What other motive could have prompted choice ?

Therefore be peace again : exult, ye hills !
Ye vales rejoicingly break forth in song !   1375
Incipe, parve puer, begin, small boy,
Risu cognoscere patrem, with a laugh
To recognize thy parent !   Nor do thou

Boggle, oh parent, to return the grace!
Nec anceps hære, pater, puero   1380
Cognoscendo—one may well eke out the prayer!
In vain!   The perverse Guido doubts his eyes,
Distrusts assurance, lets the devil drive.
Because his house is swept and garnished now,
He, having summoned seven like himself,   1385
Must hurry thither, knock and enter in,
And make the last worse than the first, indeed!
Is he content?   We are.   No further blame
O' the man and murder!   They were stigmatized
Befittingly : the Court heard long ago   1390
My mind o' the matter, which, outpouring full,
Has long since swept like surge, i' the simile
Of Homer, overborne both dyke and dam,
And whelmed alike client and advocate :
His fate is sealed, his life as good as gone,   1395
On him I am not tempted to waste word.
Yet though my purpose holds,—which was and is
And solely shall be to the very end,
To draw the true *effigies* of a saint,
Do justice to perfection in the sex,—   1400
Yet let not some gross pamperer of the flesh
And niggard in the spirit's nourishment,
Whose feeding hath offuscated his wit
Rather than law,—he never had, to lose—

Let not such advocate object to me   1405
I leave my proper function of attack !
"What 's this to Bacchus?"—(in the classic phrase,
Well used, for once) he hiccups probably.
O Advocate o' the Poor, thou born to make
Their blessing void—*beati pauperes!*   1410
By painting saintship I depicture sin :
Beside my pearl, I prove how black thy jet,
And, through Pompilia's virtue, Guido's crime.

Back to her, then,—with but one beauty more,
End we our argument,—one crowning grace   1415
Pre-eminent 'mid agony and death.
For to the last Pompilia played her part,
Used the right means to the permissible end,
And, wily as an eel that stirs the mud
Thick overhead, so baffling spearman's thrust, 1420
She, while he stabbed her, simulated death,
Delayed, for his sake, the catastrophe,
Obtained herself a respite, four days' grace,
Whereby she told her story to the world,
Enabled me to make the present speech,   1425
And, by a full confession, saved her soul.

Yet hold, even here would malice leer its last,
Gurgle its choked remonstrance : snake, hiss free !

Oh, that 's the objection?   And to whom?—not her
But me, forsooth—as, in the very act   1430
Of both confession and (what followed close)
Subsequent talk, chatter and gossipry,
Babble to sympathizing he and she
Whoever chose besiege her dying bed,—
As this were found at variance with my tale,   1435
Falsified all I have adduced for truth,
Admitted not one peccadillo here,
Pretended to perfection, first and last,
O' the whole procedure—perfect in the end,
Perfect i' the means, perfect in everything,   1440
Leaving a lawyer nothing to excuse,
Reason away and show his skill about !
—A flight, impossible to Adamic flesh,
Just to be fancied, scarcely to be wished,
And, anyhow, unpleadable in court !   1445
" How reconcile," gasps Malice, "that with this? "

Your "this," friend, is extraneous to the law,
Comes of men's outside meddling, the unskilled
Interposition of such fools as press
Out of their province.   Must I speak my mind?   1450
Far better had Pompilia died o' the spot
Than found a tongue to wag and shame the law,
Shame most of all herself,—could friendship fail

And advocacy lie less on the alert :
But no, they shall protect her to the end !   1455
Do I credit the alleged narration?   No !
Lied our Pompilia then, to laud herself?
Still, no !   Clear up what seems discrepancy?
The means abound : art 's long, though time is short ;
So, keeping me in compass, all I urge   1460
Is—since, confession at the point of death,
Nam in articulo mortis, with the Church
Passes for statement honest and sincere,
Nemo presumitur reus esse,—then,
If sure that all affirmed would be believed,   1465
'T was charity, in her so circumstanced,
To spend the last breath in one effort more
For universal good of friend and foe :
And,—by pretending utter innocence,
Nay, freedom from each foible we forgive,—   1470
Re-integrate—not solely her own fame,
But do the like kind office for the priest
Whom telling the crude truth about might vex,
Haply expose to peril, abbreviate
Indeed the long career of usefulness   1475
Presumably before him : while her lord,
Whose fleeting life is forfeit to the law,—
What mercy to the culprit if, by just
The gift of such a full certificate

Of his immitigable guiltiness,   1480
She stifled in him the absurd conceit
Of murder as it were a mere revenge
—Stopped confirmation of that jealousy
Which, did she but acknowledge the first flaw,
The faintest foible, had emboldened him   1485
To battle with the charge, baulk penitence,
Bar preparation for impending fate!
Whereas, persuade him that he slew a saint
Who sinned not even where she may have sinned,
You urge him all the brisklier to repent   1490
Of most and least and aught and everything!
Still, if this view of mine content you not,
Lords, nor excuse the genial falsehood here,
We come to our *Triarii*, last resource:
We fall back on the inexpugnable,   1495
Submitting,—she confessed before she talked!
The sacrament obliterates the sin:
What is not,—was not, therefore, in a sense.
Let Molinists distinguish, " Souls washed white
" But red once, still show pinkish to the eye!" 1500
We say, abolishment is nothingness,
And nothingness has neither head nor tail,
End nor beginning!   Better estimate
Exorbitantly, than disparage aught
Of the efficacity of the act, I hope!   1505

Solvuntur tabulæ?   May we laugh and go?
Well,—not before (in filial gratitude
To Law, who, mighty mother, waves adieu)
We take on us to vindicate Law's self !
For,—yea, Sirs,—curb the start, curtail the stare !—
Remains that we apologize for haste   1511
I' the Law, our lady who here bristles up
" Blame my procedure?   Could the Court mistake?
" (Which were indeed a misery to think)
" Did not my sentence in the former stage   1515
" O' the business bear a title plain enough?
" *Decretum* "—I translate it word for word—
" ' Decreed : the priest, for his complicity
" ' I' the flight and deviation of the dame,
" ' As well as for unlawful intercourse,   1520
" ' Is banished three years : ' crime and penalty,
" Declared alike.   If he be taxed with guilt,
" How can you call Pompilia innocent?
" If both be innocent, have I been just? "

Gently, O mother, judge men—whose mistake 1525
Is in the mere misapprehensiveness !
The *Titulus* a-top of your decree
Was but to ticket there the kind of charge
You in good time would arbitrate upon.
Title is one thing,—arbitration's self,   1530

Probatio, quite another possibly.
Subsistit, there holds good the old response,
Responsio tradita, we must not stick,
Quod non sit attendendus Titulus,
To the Title, *sed Probatio*, but the Proof,   1535
Resultans ex processu, the result
O' the Trial, and the style of punishment,
Et pœna per sententiam imposita.
All is tentative, till the sentence come:
An indication of what men expect,   1540
But nowise an assurance they shall find.
Lords, what if we permissibly relax
The tense bow, as the law-god Phœbus bids,
Relieve our gravity at labour's close?
I traverse Rome, feel thirsty, need a draught,   1545
Look for a wine-shop, find it by the bough
Projecting as to say " Here wine is sold ! "
So much I know,—" sold : " but what sort of wine?
Strong, weak, sweet, sour, home-made or foreign drink?
That much must I discover by myself.   1550
" Wine is sold," quoth the bough, " but good or bad,
" Find, and inform us when you smack your lips ! "
Exactly so, Law hangs her title forth,
To show she entertains you with such case
About such crime.   Come in ! she pours, you quaff.
You find the Priest good liquor in the main,   1556

But heady and provocative of brawls :
Remand the residue to flask once more,
Lay it low where it may deposit lees,
I' the cellar : thence produce it presently,   1560
Three years the brighter and the better !

                                                                     Thus,
Law's son, have I bestowed my filial help,
And thus I end, *tenax proposito ;*
Point to point as I purposed have I drawn   1565
Pompilia, and implied as terribly
Guido : so, gazing, let the world crown Law—
Able once more, despite my impotence,
And helped by the acumen of the Court,
To eliminate, display, make triumph truth !   1570
What other prize than truth were worth the pains ?

There 's my oration—much exceeds in length
That famed panegyric of Isocrates,
They say it took him fifteen years to pen.
But all those ancients could say anything !   1575
He put in just what rushed into his head :
While I shall have to prune and pare and print.
This comes of being born in modern times
With priests for auditory.   Still, it pays.

X.

THE POPE.

LIKE to Ahasuerus, that shrewd prince,
I will begin,—as is, these seven years now,
My daily wont,—and read a History
(Written by one whose deft right hand was dust
To the last digit, ages ere my birth)   5
Of all my predecessors, Popes of Rome :
For though mine ancient early dropped the pen,
Yet others picked it up and wrote it dry,
Since of the making books there is no end.
And so I have the Papacy complete   10
From Peter first to Alexander last;
Can question each and take instruction so.
Have I to dare?—I ask, how dared this Pope?
To suffer?—Suchanone, how suffered he?
Being about to judge, as now, I seek   15
How judged once, well or ill, some other Pope;
Study some signal judgment that subsists

To blaze on, or else blot, the page which seals
The sum up of what gain or loss to God
Came of His one more Vicar in the world.   20
So, do I find example, rule of life;
So, square and set in order the next page,
Shall be stretched smooth o'er my own funeral cyst.

Eight hundred years exact before the year
I was made Pope, men made Formosus Pope,   25
Say Sigebert and other chroniclers.
Ere I confirm or quash the Trial here
Of Guido Franceschini and his friends,
Read,—How there was a ghastly Trial once
Of a dead man by a live man, and both, Popes: 30
Thus—in the antique penman's very phrase.

" Then Stephen, Pope and seventh of the name,
" Cried out, in synod as he sat in state,
" While choler quivered on his brow and beard,
" ' Come into court, Formosus, thou lost wretch, 35
" ' That claimedst to be late Pope as even I!'

" And at the word the great door of the church
" Flew wide, and in they brought Formosus' self,
" The body of him, dead, even as embalmed
" And buried duly in the Vatican   40

X.   F

" Eight months before, exhumed thus for the nonce.
" They set it, that dead body of a Pope,
" Clothed in pontific vesture now again,
" Upright on Peter's chair as if alive.

" And Stephen, springing up, cried furiously   45
" ' Bishop of Porto, wherefore didst presume
" ' To leave that see and take this Roman see,
" ' Exchange the lesser for the greater see,
" ' —A thing against the canons of the Church?'

" Then one—(a Deacon who, observing forms,   50
" Was placed by Stephen to repel the charge,
" Be advocate and mouthpiece of the corpse)—
" Spoke as he dared, set stammeringly forth
" With white lips and dry tongue,—as but a youth,
" For frightful was the corpse-face to behold,—   55
" How nowise lacked there precedent for this.

" But when, for his last precedent of all,
" Emboldened by the Spirit, out he blurts
" ' And, Holy Father, didst not thou thyself
" ' Vacate the lesser for the greater see,   60
" ' Half a year since change Arago for Rome?'
" ' —Ye have the sin's defence now, Synod mine!'
" Shrieks Stephen in a beastly froth of rage :

" ' Judge now betwixt him dead and me alive !

" ' Hath he intruded, or do I pretend ?   65

" ' Judge, judge ! '—breaks wavelike one whole foam of
     wrath.

" Whereupon they, being friends and followers,

" Said ' Ay, thou art Christ's Vicar, and not he !

" ' Away with what is frightful to behold !

" ' This act was uncanonic and a fault.'   70

" Then, swallowed up in rage, Stephen exclaimed

" ' So, guilty ! So, remains I punish guilt !

" ' He is unpoped, and all he did I damn :

" ' The Bishop, that ordained him, I degrade :

" ' Depose to laics those he raised to priests :   75

" ' What they have wrought is mischief nor shall stand,

" ' It is confusion, let it vex no more !

" ' Since I revoke, annul and abrogate

" ' All his decrees in all kinds : they are void !

" ' In token whereof and warning to the world,   80

" ' Strip me yon miscreant of those robes usurped,

" ' And clothe him with vile serge befitting such !

" ' Then hale the carrion to the market-place :

" ' Let the town-hangman chop from his right hand

" ' Those same three fingers which he blessed withal ; 85

" ' Next cut the head off once was crowned forsooth :

" ' And last go fling them, fingers, head and trunk,
" '.To Tiber that my Christian fish may sup!'
" —Either because of ΙΧΘΥΣ which means Fish
" And very aptly symbolizes Christ,   90
" Or else because the Pope is Fisherman,
" And seals with Fisher's-signet.

                              " Anyway,
" So said, so done : himself, to see it done,
" Followed the corpse they trailed from street to street
" Till into Tiber wave they threw the thing.   96
" The people, crowded on the banks to see,
" Were loud or mute, wept or laughed, cursed or jeered,
" According as the deed addressed their sense ;
" A scandal verily : and out spake a Jew   100
" ' Wot ye your Christ had vexed our Herod thus? '

" Now when, Formosus being dead a year,
" His judge Pope Stephen tasted death in turn,
" Made captive by the mob and strangled straight,
" Romanus, his successor for a month,   105
" Did make protest Formosus was with God,
" Holy, just, true in thought and word and deed.
" Next Theodore, who reigned but twenty days,
" Therein convoked a synod, whose decree
" Did reinstate, repope the late unpoped,   110

" And do away with Stephen as accursed.

" So that when presently certain fisher-folk

" (As if the queasy river could not hold

" Its swallowed Jonas, but discharged the meal)

" Produced the timely product of their nets, 115

" The mutilated man, Formosus,—saved

" From putrefaction by the embalmer's spice,

" Or, as some said, by sanctity of flesh,—

" ' Why, lay the body again,' bade Theodore,

" ' Among his predecessors, in the church 120

" ' And burial-place of Peter !' which was done.

" ' And,' addeth Luitprand, 'many of repute,

" ' Pious and still alive, avouch to me

" ' That, as they bore the body up the aisle,

" ' The saints in imaged row bowed each his head 125

" ' For welcome to a brother-saint come back.'

" As for Romanus and this Theodore,

" These two Popes, through the brief reign granted each,

" Could but initiate what John came to close

" And give the final stamp to : he it was 130

" Ninth of the name, (I follow the best guides)

" Who,—in full synod at Ravenna held

" With Bishops seventy-four, and present too

" Eude King of France with his Archbishopry,—

" Did condemn Stephen, anathematize 135

" The disinterment, and make all blots blank,

" ' For,' argueth here Auxilius in a place
" *De Ordinationibus*, ' precedents
" ' Had been, no lack, before Formosus long,
" ' Of Bishops so transferred from see to see,—   140
" ' Marinus, for example : ' read the tract.

" But, after John, came Sergius, reaffirmed
" The right of Stephen, cursed Formosus, nay
" Cast out, some say, his corpse a second time.
" And here,— because the matter went to ground, 145
" Fretted by new griefs, other cares of the age,—
" Here is the last pronouncing of the Church,
" Her sentence that subsists unto this day.
" Yet constantly opinion hath prevailed
" I' the Church, Formosus was a holy man."   150

Which of the judgments was infallible?
Which of my predecessors spoke for God?
And what availed Formosus that this cursed,
That blessed, and then this other cursed again?
" Fear ye not those whose power can kill the body 155
" And not the soul," saith Christ, " but rather those
" Can cast both soul and body into hell ! "

John judged thus in Eight Hundred Ninety Eight,
Exact eight hundred years ago to-day

When, sitting in his stead, Vice-gerent here,   160
I must give judgment on my own behoof.
So worked the predecessor : now, my turn !

In God's name !   Once more on this earth of God's,
While twilight lasts and time wherein to work,
I take His staff with my uncertain hand,   165
And stay my six and fourscore years, my due
Labour and sorrow, on His judgment-seat,
And forthwith think, speak, act, in place of Him—
The Pope for Christ.   Once more appeal is made
From man's assize to mine : I sit and see   170
Another poor weak trembling human wretch
Pushed by his fellows, who pretend the right,
Up to the gulf which, where I gaze, begins
From this world to the next,—gives way and way,
Just on the edge over the awful dark :   175
With nothing to arrest him but my feet.
He catches at me with convulsive face,
Cries "Leave to live the natural minute more !"
While hollowly the avengers echo "Leave?
"None ! So has he exceeded man's due share   180
"In man's fit license, wrung by Adam's fall,
"To sin and yet not surely die,—that we,
"All of us sinful, all with need of grace,
"All chary of our life,—the minute more

"Or minute less of grace which saves a soul,—   185
"Bound to make common cause with who craves time,
"—We yet protest against the exorbitance
"Of sin in this one sinner, and demand
"That his poor sole remaining piece of time
"Be plucked from out his clutch : put him to death !
"Punish him now !   As for the weal or woe   191
"Hereafter, God grant mercy !   Man be just,
"Nor let the felon boast he went scot-free !"
And I am bound, the solitary judge,
To weigh the worth, decide upon the plea,   195
And either hold a hand out, or withdraw
A foot and let the wretch drift to the fall.
Ay, and while thus I dally, dare perchance
Put fancies for a comfort 'twixt this calm
And yonder passion that I have to bear,—   200
As if reprieve were possible for both
Prisoner and Pope,—how easy were reprieve !
A touch o' the hand-bell here, a hasty word
To those who wait, and wonder they wait long,
I' the passage there, and I should gain the life !—
Yea, though I flatter me with fancy thus,   206
I know it is but nature's craven-trick.
The case is over, judgment at an end,
And all things done now and irrevocable :
A mere dead man is Franceschini here,   210

Even as Formosus centuries ago.
I have worn through this sombre wintry day,
With winter in my soul beyond the world's,
Over these dismalest of documents
Which drew night down on me ere eve befell,— 215
Pleadings and counter-pleadings, figure of fact
Beside fact's self, these summaries to-wit,—
How certain three were slain by certain five :
I read here why it was, and how it went,
And how the chief o' the five preferred excuse, 220
And how law rather chose defence should lie,—
What argument he urged by wary word
When free to play off wile, start subterfuge,
And what the unguarded groan told, torture's feat
When law grew brutal, outbroke, overbore 225
And glutted hunger on the truth, at last,—
No matter for the flesh and blood between.
All 's a clear rede and no more riddle now.
Truth, nowhere, lies yet everywhere in these—
Not absolutely in a portion, yet 230
Evolvible from the whole : evolved at last
Painfully, held tenaciously by me.
Therefore there is not any doubt to clear
When I shall write the brief word presently
And chink the hand-bell, which I pause to do. 235
Irresolute ? Not I, more than the mound

With the pine-trees on it yonder! Some surmise,
Perchance, that since man's wit is fallible,
Mine may fail here? Suppose it so,—what then?
Say,—Guido, I count guilty, there 's no babe   240
So guiltless, for I misconceive the man !
What 's in the chance should move me from my mind?
If, as I walk in a rough country-side,
Peasants of mine cry " Thou art he can help,
" Lord of the land and counted wise to boot: 245
" Look at our brother, strangling in his foam,
" He fell so where we find him,—prove thy worth ! "
I may presume, pronounce, " A frenzy-fit,
" A falling-sickness or a fever-stroke !
" Breathe a vein, copiously let blood at once ! "   250
So perishes the patient, and anon
I hear my peasants—" All was error, lord !
" Our story, thy prescription : for there crawled
" In due time from our hapless brother's breast
" The serpent which had stung him : bleeding slew
" Whom a prompt cordial had restored to health." 256
What other should I say than " God so willed :
" Mankind is ignorant, a man am I :
" Call ignorance my sorrow, not my sin ! "
So and not otherwise, in after-time,   260
If some acuter wit, fresh probing, sound
This multifarious mass of words and deeds

Deeper, and reach through guilt to innocence,
I shall face Guido's ghost nor blench a jot.
"God who set me to judge thee, meted out   265
"So much of judging faculty, no more :
"Ask Him if I was slack in use thereof ! "
I hold a heavier fault imputable
Inasmuch as I changed a chaplain once,
For no cause,—no, if I must bare my heart,—   270
Save that he snuffled somewhat saying mass.
For I am ware it is the seed of act,
God holds appraising in His hollow palm,
Not act grown great thence on the world below,
Leafage and branchage, vulgar eyes admire.   275
Therefore I stand on my integrity,
Nor fear at all : and if I hesitate,
It is because I need to breathe awhile,
Rest, as the human right allows, review
Intent the little seeds of act, my tree,—   280
The thought, which, clothed in deed, I give the world
At chink of bell and push of arrased door.

O pale departure, dim disgrace of day !
Winter 's in wane, his vengeful worst art thou,
To dash the boldness of advancing March !   285
Thy chill persistent rain has purged our streets
Of gossipry ; pert tongue and idle ear

By this, consort 'neath archway, portico.
But wheresoe'er Rome gathers in the grey,   289
Two names now snap and flash from mouth to mouth—
(Sparks, flint and steel strike) Guido and the Pope.
By this same hour to-morrow eve—aha,
How do they call him?—the sagacious Swede
Who finds by figures how the chances prove,
Why one comes rather than another thing,   295
As, say, such dots turn up by throw of dice,
Or, if we dip in Virgil here and there
And prick for such a verse, when such shall point.
Take this Swede, tell him, hiding name and rank,
Two men are in our city this dull eve;   300
One doomed to death,—but hundreds in such plight
Slip aside, clean escape by leave of law
Which leans to mercy in this latter time;
Moreover in the plenitude of life
Is he, with strength of limb and brain adroit,   305
Presumably of service here: beside,
The man is noble, backed by nobler friends:
Nay, they so wish him well, the city's self
Makes common cause with who—house-magistrate,
Patron of hearth and home, domestic lord—   310
But ruled his own, let aliens cavil.   Die?
He 'll bribe a gaoler or break prison first!
Nay, a sedition may be helpful, give

Hint to the mob to batter wall, burn gate,
And bid the favourite malefactor march.   315
Calculate now these chances of escape !
" It is not probable, but well may be."
Again, there is another man, weighed now
By twice eight years beyond the seven-times-ten,
Appointed overweight to break our branch.   320
And this man's loaded branch lifts, more than snow,
All the world's cark and care, though a bird's nest
Were a superfluous burthen : notably
Hath he been pressed, as if his age were youth,
From to-day's dawn till now that day departs,   325
Trying one question with true sweat of soul
" Shall the said doomed man fitlier die or live ? "
When a straw swallowed in his posset, stool
Stumbled on where his path lies, any puff
That 's incident to such a smoking flax,   330
Hurries the natural end and quenches him !
Now calculate, thou sage, the chances here,
Say, which shall die the sooner, this or that?
" That, possibly, this in all likelihood."
I thought so : yet thou tripp'st, my foreign friend ! 335
No, it will be quite otherwise,—to-day
Is Guido's last : my term is yet to run.

But say the Swede were right, and I forthwith

Acknowledge a prompt summons and lie dead :
Why, then I stand already in God's face   34c
And hear " Since by its fruit a tree is judged,
" Show me thy fruit, the latest act of thine !
" For in the last is summed the first and all,—
" What thy life last put heart and soul into,
" There shall I taste thy product." I must plead 345
This condemnation of a man to-day.

Not so ! Expect nor question nor reply
At what we figure as God's judgment-bar !
None of this vile way by the barren words
Which, more than any deed, characterize   350
Man as made subject to a curse : no speech—
That still bursts o'er some lie which lurks inside,
As the split skin across the coppery snake,
And most denotes man ! since, in all beside,
In hate or lust or guile or unbelief,   355
Out of some core of truth the excrescence comes,
And, in the last resort, the man may urge
" So was I made, a weak thing that gave way
" To truth, to impulse only strong since true,
" And hated, lusted, used guile, forwent faith." 360
But when man walks the garden of this world
For his own solace, and, unchecked by law,   /
Speaks or keeps silence as himself sees fit,

Without the least incumbency to lie,
—Why, can he tell you what a rose is like,   365
Or how the birds fly, and not slip to false
Though truth serve better? / Man must tell his mate
Of you, me and himself, knowing he lies,
Knowing his fellow knows the same,—will think
" He lies, it is the method of a man ! "   370
And yet will speak for answer " It is truth "
To him who shall rejoin " Again a lie ! '
Therefore these filthy rags of speech, this coil
Of statement, comment, query and response,
Tatters all too contaminate for use,   375
Have no renewing : He, the Truth, is, too,
The Word.   We men, in our degree, may know
There, simply, instantaneously, as here
After long time and amid many lies,
Whatever we dare think we know indeed   380
—That I am I, as He is He,—what else ?
But be man's method for man's life at least !
Wherefore, Antonio Pignatelli, thou
My ancient self, who wast no Pope so long
But studiedst God and man, the many years   385
I' the school, i' the cloister, in the diocese
Domestic, legate-rule in foreign lands,—
Thou other force in those old busy days
Than this grey ultimate decrepitude,—

Yet sensible of fires that more and more   390
Visit a soul, in passage to the sky,
Left nakeder than when flesh-robe was new—
Thou, not Pope but the mere old man o' the world,
Supposed inquisitive and dispassionate,
Wilt thou, the one whose speech I somewhat trust,
Question the after-me, this self now Pope,   396
Hear his procedure, criticize his work?
Wise in its generation is the world.

This is why Guido is found reprobate.
I see him furnished forth for his career,   400
On starting for the life-chance in our world,
With nearly all we count sufficient help:
Body and mind in balance, a sound frame,
A solid intellect: the wit to seek,
Wisdom to choose, and courage wherewithal   405
To deal in whatsoever circumstance
Should minister to man, make life succeed.
Oh, and much drawback! what were earth without?
Is this our ultimate stage, or starting-place
To try man's foot, if it will creep or climb,   410
'Mid obstacles in seeming, points that prove
Advantage for who vaults from low to high
And makes the stumbling-block a stepping-stone?
So, Guido, born with appetite, lacks food:

Is poor, who yet could deftly play-off wealth :   415
Straitened, whose limbs are restless till at large.
He, as he eyes each outlet of the cirque
And narrow penfold for probation, pines
After the good things just outside its grate,
With less monition, fainter conscience-twitch,   420
Rarer instinctive qualm at the first feel
Of greed unseemly, prompting grasp undue,
Than nature furnishes her main mankind,—
Making it harder to do wrong than right
The first time, careful lest the common ear   425
Break measure, miss the outstep of life's march.
Wherein I see a trial fair and fit
For one else too unfairly fenced about,
Set above sin, beyond his fellows here :
Guarded from the arch-tempter all must fight,   430
By a great birth, traditionary name,
Diligent culture, choice companionship,
Above all, conversancy with the faith
Which puts forth for its base of doctrine just
" Man is born nowise to content himself,   435
" But please God."   He accepted such a rule,
Recognized man's obedience ; and the Church,
Which simply is such rule's embodiment,
He clave to, he held on by,—nay, indeed,
Near pushed inside of, deep as layman durst,   440

X.   G

Professed so much of priesthood as might sue
For priest's-exemption where the layman sinned,—
Got his arm frocked which, bare, the law would bruise.
Hence, at this moment, what 's his last resource,
His extreme stay and utmost stretch of hope   445
But that,—convicted of such crime as law
Wipes not away save with a worldling's blood,—
Guido, the three-parts consecrate, may 'scape?
Nay, the portentous brothers of the man
Are veritably priests, protected each ·   450
May do his murder in the Church's pale,
Abate Paul, Canon Girolamo !
This is the man proves irreligiousest
Of all mankind, religion's parasite !
This may forsooth plead dinned ear, jaded sense, 455
The vice o' the watcher who bides near the bell,
Sleeps sound because the clock is vigilant,
And cares not whether it be shade or shine,
Doling out day and night to all men else !
Why was the choice o' the man to niche himself   460
Perversely 'neath the tower where Time's own tongue
Thus undertakes to sermonize the world?
Why, but because the solemn is safe too,
The belfry proves a fortress of a sort,
Has other uses than to teach the hour: 465
Turns sunscreen, paravent and ombrifuge

To whoso seeks a shelter in its pale,
—Ay, and attractive to unwary folk
Who gaze at storied portal, statued spire,
And go home with full head but empty purse,   470
Nor dare suspect the sacristan the thief!
Shall Judas,—hard upon the donor's heel,
To filch the fragments of the basket,—plead
He was too near the preacher's mouth, nor sat
Attent with fifties in a company?   475
No,—closer to promulgated decree,
Clearer the censure of default.   Proceed!

I find him bound, then, to begin life well;
Fortified by propitious circumstance,
Great birth, good breeding, with the Church for guide,
How lives he?   Cased thus in a coat of proof,   481
Mailed like a man-at-arms, though all the while
A puny starveling,—does the breast pant big,
The limb swell to the limit, emptiness
Strive to become solidity indeed?   485
Rather, he shrinks up like the ambiguous fish,
Detaches flesh from shell and outside show,
And steals by moonlight (I have seen the thing)
In and out, now to prey and now to skulk.
Armour he boasts when a wave breaks on beach,   490
Or bird stoops for the prize: with peril nigh,—

The man of rank, the much-befriended-man,
The man almost affiliate to the Church,
Such is to deal with, let the world beware!
Does the world recognize, pass prudently?   495
Do tides abate and sea-fowl hunt i' the deep?
Already is the slug from out its mew,
Ignobly faring with all loose and free,
Sand-fly and slush-worm at their garbage-feast,
A naked blotch no better than they all: 500
Guido has dropped nobility, slipped the Church,
Plays trickster if not cut-purse, body and soul
Prostrate among the filthy feeders—faugh!
And when Law takes him by surprise at last,
Catches the foul thing on its carrion-prey,   505
Behold, he points to shell left high and dry,
Pleads "But the case out yonder is myself!"
Nay, it is thou, Law prongs amid thy peers,
Congenial vermin; that was none of thee,
Thine outside,—give it to the soldier-crab!   510

For I find this black mark impinge the man,
That he believes in just the vile of life.
Low instinct, base pretension, are these truth?
Then, that aforesaid armour, probity
He figures in, is falsehood scale on scale;   515
Honour and faith,—a lie and a disguise,

Probably for all livers in this world,
Certainly for himself! All say good words
To who will hear, all do thereby bad deeds
To who must undergo; so thrive mankind!   520
See this habitual creed exemplified
Most in the last deliberate act; as last,
So, very sum and substance of the soul
Of him that planned and leaves one perfect piece,
The sin brought under jurisdiction now,   525
Even the marriage of the man : this act
I sever from his life as sample, show
For Guido's self, intend to test him by,
As, from a cup filled fairly at the fount,
By the components we decide enough   530
Or to let flow as late, or staunch the source.

He purposes this marriage, I remark,
On no one motive that should prompt thereto—
Farthest, by consequence, from ends alleged
Appropriate to the action ; so they were :   535
The best, he knew and feigned, the worst he took.
Not one permissible impulse moves the man,
From the mere liking of the eye and ear,
To the true longing of the heart that loves,
No trace of these : but all to instigate,   540
Is what sinks man past level of the brute

Whose appetite if brutish is a truth.
All is the lust for money : to get gold,—
Why, lie, rob, if it must be, murder !   Make
Body and soul wring gold out, lured within   545
The clutch of hate by love, the trap's pretence !
What good else get from bodies and from souls ?
This got, there were some life to lead thereby,
—What, where or how, appreciate those who tell
How the toad lives : it lives,—enough for me !   550
To get this good,—with but a groan or so,
Then, silence of the victims,—were the feat.
He foresaw, made a picture in his mind,—
Of father and mother stunned and echoless
To the blow, as they lie staring at fate's jaws   555
Their folly danced into, till the woe fell ;
Edged in a month by strenuous cruelty
From even the poor nook whence they watched the wolf
Feast on their heart, the lamb-like child his prey ;
Plundered to the last remnant of their wealth,   560
(What daily pittance pleased the plunderer dole)
Hunted forth to go hide head, starve and die,
And leave the pale awe-stricken wife, past hope
Of help i' the world now, mute and motionless,
His slave, his chattel, to first use, then destroy.   565
All this, he bent mind how to bring about,
Put plain in act and life, as painted plain,

Sò have success, reach crown of earthly good,
In this particular enterprise of man,
By marriage—undertaken in God's face   570
With all these lies so opposite God's truth,
For end so other than man's end.

                              Thus schemes
Guido, and thus would carry out his scheme :
But when an obstacle first blocks the path,   575
When he finds none may boast monopoly
Of lies and trick i' the tricking lying world,—
That sorry timid natures, even this sort
O' the Comparini, want nor trick nor lie
Proper to the kind,—that as the gor-crow treats 580
The bramble-finch so treats the finch the moth,
And the great Guido is minutely matched
By this same couple,—whether true or false
The revelation of Pompilia's birth,
Which in a moment brings his scheme to nought,—
Then, he is piqued, advances yet a stage,   586
Leaves the low region to the finch and fly,·
Soars to the zenith whence the fiercer fowl
May dare the inimitable swoop.   I see.
He draws now on the curious crime, the fine   590
Felicity and flower of wickedness ;
Determines, by the utmost exercise

Of violence, made safe and sure by craft,
To satiate malice, pluck one last arch-pang
From the parents, else would triumph out of reach, 595
By punishing their child, within reach yet,
Who, by thought, word or deed, could nowise wrong
I' the matter that now moves him.   So plans he,
Always subordinating (note the point!)
Revenge, the manlier sin, to interest   600
The meaner,—would pluck pang forth, but unclench
No gripe in the act, let fall no money-piece.
Hence a plan for so plaguing, body and soul,
His wife, so putting, day by day, hour by hour,
The untried torture to the untouched place,   605
As must precipitate an end foreseen,
Goad her into some plain revolt, most like
Plunge upon patent suicidal shame,
Death to herself, damnation by rebound
To those whose hearts he, holding hers, holds still:
Such plan as, in its bad completeness, shall   611
Ruin the three together and alike,
Yet leave himself in luck and liberty,
No claim renounced, no right a forfeiture,
His person unendangered, his good fame   615
Without a flaw, his pristine worth intact,—
While they, with all their claims and rights that cling,
Shall forthwith crumble off him every side,

Scorched into dust, a plaything for the winds.
As when, in our Campagna, there is fired   620
The nest-like work that overruns a hut;
And, as the thatch burns here, there, everywhere,
Even to the ivy and wild vine, that bound
And blessed the home where men were happy once,
There rises gradual, black amid the blaze,   625
Some grim and unscathed nucleus of the nest,—
Some old malicious tower, some obscene tomb
They thought a temple in their ignorance,
And clung about and thought to lean upon—
There laughs it o'er their ravage,—where are they?
So did his cruelty burn life about,   631
And lay the ruin bare in dreadfulness,   '
Try the persistency of torment so
Upon the wife, that, at extremity,
Some crisis brought about by fire and flame,   635
The patient frenzy-stung must needs break loose,
Fly anyhow, find refuge anywhere,
Even in the arms of who should front her first,
No monster but a man—while nature shrieked
" Or thus escape, or die ! "   The spasm arrived,   640
Not the escape by way of sin,—O God,
Who shall pluck sheep Thou holdest, from Thy hand?
Therefore she lay resigned to die,—so far
The simple cruelty was foiled.   Why then,

Craft to the rescue, let craft supplement   645
Cruelty and show hell a masterpiece !
Hence this consummate lie, this love-intrigue,
Unmanly simulation of a sin,
With place and time and circumstance to suit—
These letters false beyond all forgery—   650
Not just handwriting and mere authorship,
But false to body and soul they figure forth—
As though the man had cut out shape and shape
From fancies of that other Aretine,
To paste below—incorporate the filth   655
With cherub faces on a missal-page !

Whereby the man so far attains his end
That strange temptation is permitted,—see !
Pompilia wife, and Caponsacchi priest,
Are brought together as nor priest nor wife   660
Should stand, and there is passion in the place,
Power in the air for evil as for good,
Promptings from heaven and hell, as if the stars
Fought in their courses for a fate to be.
Thus stand the wife and priest, a spectacle,   665
I doubt not, to unseen assemblage there.
No lamp will mark that window for a shrine,
No tablet signalize the terrace, teach
New generations which succeed the old

The pavement of the street is holy ground;   670
No bard describe in verse how Christ prevailed
And Satan fell like lightning ! Why repine?
What does the world, told truth, but lie the more?

A second time the plot is foiled; nor, now,
By corresponding sin for countercheck,   675
No wile and trick that baffle trick and wile,—
The play o' the parents ! Here the blot is blanched
By God's gift of a purity of soul
That will not take pollution, ermine-like
Armed from dishonour by its own soft snow.   680
Such was this gift of God who showed for once
How He would have the world go white : it seems
As a new attribute were born of each
Champion of truth, the priest and wife I praise,—
As a new safeguard sprang up in defence   685
Of their new noble nature : so a thorn
Comes to the aid of and completes the rose—
Courage to-wit, no woman's gift nor priest's,
I' the crisis ; might leaps vindicating right.
See how the strong aggressor, bad and bold,   690
With every vantage, preconcerts surprise,
Leaps of a sudden at his victim's throat
In a byeway,—how fares he when face to face
With Caponsacchi? Who fights, who fears now? 694

There quails Count Guido armed to the chattering teeth,
Cowers at the steadfast eye and quiet word
O' the Canon of the Pieve !   There skulks crime
Behind law called in to back cowardice :
While out of the poor trampled worm the wife,
Springs up a serpent !   700

                    But anon of these.
Him I judge now,—of him proceed to note,
Failing the first, a second chance befriends
Guido, gives pause ere punishment arrive.
The law he called, comes, hears, adjudicates,   705
Nor does amiss i' the main,—secludes the wife
From the husband, respites the oppressed one, grants
Probation to the oppressor, could he know
The mercy of a minute's fiery purge !
The furnace-coals alike of public scorn,   710
Private remorse, heaped glowing on his head,
What if,—the force and guile, the ore's alloy,
Eliminate, his baser soul refined—
The lost be saved even yet, so as by fire ?
Let him, rebuked, go softly all his days   715
And, when no graver musings claim their due,
Meditate on a man's immense mistake
Who, fashioned to use feet and walk, deigns crawl—
Takes the unmanly means—ay, though to ends

Man scarce should make for, would but reach thro'
    wrong,— 720
May sin, but nowise needs shame manhood so :
Since fowlers hawk, shoot, nay and snare the game,
And yet eschew vile practice, nor find sport
In torch-light treachery or the luring owl.

But how hunts Guido ? Why, the fraudful trap— 725
Late spurned to ruin by the indignant feet
Of fellows in the chase who loved fair play—
Here he picks up its fragments to the least,
Lades him and hies to the old lurking-place
Where haply he may patch again, refit 730
The mischief, file its blunted teeth anew,
Make sure, next time, first snap shall break the bone.
Craft, greed and violence complot revenge :
Craft, for its quota, schemes to bring about
And seize occasion and be safe withal : 735
Greed craves its act may work both far and near,
Crush the tree, branch and trunk and root, beside.
Whichever twig or leaf arrests a streak
Of possible sunshine else would coin itself,
And drop down one more gold piece in the path :
Violence stipulates " Advantage proved 741
" And safety sure, be pain the overplus !
" Murder with jagged knife ! Cut but tear too !

" Foiled oft, starved long, glut malice for amends ! "
And what, craft's scheme? scheme sorrowful and strange
As though the elements, whom mercy checked,   746
Had mustered hate for one eruption more,
One final deluge to surprise the Ark
Cradled and sleeping on its mountain-top :
Their outbreak-signal—what but the dove's coo,   750
Back with the olive in her bill for news
Sorrow was over?   'T is an infant's birth,
Guido's first born, his son and heir, that gives
The occasion : other men cut free their souls
From care in such a case, fly up in thanks   755
To God, reach, recognize His love for once :
Guido cries " Soul, at last the mire is thine !
" Lie there in likeness of a money-bag
" My babe's birth so pins down past moving now,
" That I dare cut adrift the lives I late   760
" Scrupled to touch lest thou escape with them !
" These parents and their child my wife,—touch one,
" Lose all !   Their rights determined on a head
" I could but hate, not harm, since from each hair
" Dangled a hope for me : now—chance and change !
" No right was in their child but passes plain   766
" To that child's child and through such child to me.
" I am a father now,—come what, come will,
" I represent my child ; he comes between —

" Cuts sudden off the sunshine of this life　　770
" From those three: why, the gold is in his curls!
" Not with old Pietro's, Violante's head,
" Not his grey horror, her more hideous black—
" Go these, devoted to the knife! "

　　　　　　　　　　　　'T is done:　775
Wherefore should mind misgive, heart hesitate?
He calls to counsel, fashions certain four
Colourless natures counted clean till now,
—Rustic simplicity, uncorrupted youth,
Ignorant virtue! Here 's the gold o' the prime　780
When Saturn ruled, shall shock our leaden day—
The clown abash the courtier! Mark it, bards!
The courtier tries his hand on clownship·here,
Speaks a word, names a crime, appoints a price,—
Just breathes on what, suffused with all himself,　785
Is red-hot henceforth past distinction now
I' the common glow of hell. And thus they break
And blaze on us at Rome, Christ's birthnight-eve!
Oh angels that sang erst " On the earth, peace!
" To man, good will! "—such peace finds earth
　　　to-day!　　　　　　　　　　　790
After the seventeen hundred years, so man
Wills good to man, so Guido makes complete
His murder! what is it I said?—cuts loose
Three lives that hitherto he suffered cling,

Simply because each served to nail secure,   795
By a corner of the money-bag, his soul,—
Therefore, lives sacred till the babe's first breath
O'erweights them in the balance,—off they fly !

So is the murder managed, sin conceived   799
To the full : and why not crowned with triumph too?
Why must the sin, conceived thus, bring forth death?
I note how, within hair's-breadth of escape,   .
Impunity and the thing supposed success,
Guido is found when the check comes, the change,
The monitory touch o' the tether—felt   805
By few, not marked by many, named by none
At the moment, only recognized aright
I' the fulness of the days, for God's, lest sin
Exceed the service, leap the line : such check—
A secret which this life finds hard to keep,   810
And, often guessed, is never quite revealed—
Needs must trip Guido on a stumbling-block
Too vulgar, too absurdly plain i' the path !
Study this single oversight of care,
This hebetude that marred sagacity,   815
Forgetfulness of all the man best knew,—
How any stranger having need to fly,
Needs but to ask and have the means of flight.
Why, the first urchin tells you, to leave Rome,

Get horses, you must show the warrant, just   820
The banal scrap, clerk's scribble, a fair word buys,
Or foul one, if a ducat sweeten word,—
And straight authority will back demand,
Give you the pick o' the post-house !—how should he,
Then, resident at Rome for thirty years,   825
Guido, instruct a stranger !   And himself
Forgets just this poor paper scrap, wherewith
Armed, every door he knocks at opens wide
To save him : horsed and manned, with such advance
O' the hunt behind, why, 't were the easy task   830
Of hours told on the fingers of one hand,
To reach the Tuscan frontier, laugh at-home,
Light-hearted with his fellows of the place,—
Prepared by that strange shameful judgment, that
Satire upon a sentence just pronounced   835
By the Rota and confirmed by the Granduke,—
Ready in a circle to receive their peer,
Appreciate his good story how, when Rome,
The Pope-King and the populace of priests
Made common cause with their confederate   840
The other priestling who seduced his wife,
He, all unaided, wiped out the affront
With decent bloodshed and could face his friends,
Frolic it in the world's eye.   Ay, such tale
Missed such applause, and by such oversight !   845

X.   H

So, tired and footsore, those blood-flustered five
Went reeling on the road through dark and cold,
The few permissible miles, to sink at length,
Wallow and sleep in the first wayside straw,   849
As the other herd quenched, i' the wash o' the wave,
—Each swine, the devil inside him : so slept they,
And so were caught and caged—all through one trip,
One touch of fool in Guido the astute !
He curses the omission, I surmise,
More than the murder.   Why, thou fool and blind,
It is the mercy-stroke that stops thy fate,   856
Hamstrings and holds thee to thy hurt,— but how?
On the edge o' the precipice !   One minute more,
Thou hadst gone farther and fared worse, my son,
Fathoms down on the flint and fire beneath !   860
Thy comrades each and all were of one mind,
Thy murder done, to straightway murder thee
In turn, because of promised pay withheld.
So, to the last, greed found itself at odds
With craft in thee, and, proving conqueror,   865
Had sent thee, the same night that crowned thy hope,
Thither where, this same day, I see thee not,
Nor, through God's mercy, need, to-morrow, see.

Such I find Guido, midmost blotch of black
Discernible in this group of clustered crimes   870

Huddling together in the cave they call
Their palace outraged day thus penetrates.
Around him ranged, now close and now remote,
Prominent or obscure to meet the needs
O' the mage and master, I detect each shape 875
Subsidiary i' the scene nor loathed the less,
All alike coloured, all descried akin
By one and the same pitchy furnace stirred
At the centre : see, they lick the master's hand,—
This fox-faced horrible priest, this brother-brute 880
The Abate,—why, mere wolfishness looks well,
Guido stands honest in the red o' the flame,
Beside this yellow that would pass for white,
Twice Guido, all craft but no violence,
This copier of the mien and gait and garb 885
Of Peter and Paul, that he may go disguised,
Rob halt and lame, sick folk i' the temple-porch !
Armed with religion, fortified by law,
A man of peace, who trims the midnight lamp
And turns the classic page—and all for craft, 890
All to work harm with, yet incur no scratch !
While Guido brings the struggle to a close,
Paul steps back the due distance, clear o' the trap
He builds and baits.   Guido I catch and judge ;
Paul is past reach in this world and my time : 895
That is a case reserved.   Pass to the next,

H 2

The boy of the brood, the young Girolamo
Priest, Canon, and what more? nor wolf nor fox,
But hybrid, neither craft nor violence
Wholly, part violence part craft : such cross   900
Tempts speculation—will both blend one day,
And prove hell's better product?   Or subside
And let the simple quality emerge,
Go on with Satan's service the old way?
Meanwhile, what promise,—what performance too !
For there 's a new distinctive touch, I see,   906
Lust—lacking in the two—hell's own blue tint
That gives a character and marks the man
More than a match for yellow and red.   Once more,
A case reserved : why should I doubt?   Then comes
The gaunt grey nightmare in the furthest smoke,   911
The hag that gave these three abortions birth,
Unmotherly mother and unwomanly
Woman, that near turns motherhood to shame,
Womanliness to loathing : no one word,   915
No gesture to curb cruelty a whit
More than the she-pard thwarts her playsome whelps
Trying their milk-teeth on the soft o' the throat
O' the first fawn, flung, with those beseeching eyes,
Flat in the covert !   How should she but couch,   920
Lick the dry lips, unsheath the blunted claw,
Catch 'twixt her placid eyewinks at what chance

Old bloody half-forgotten dream may flit,
Born when herself was novice to the taste,
The while she lets youth take its pleasure. Last, 925
These God-abandoned wretched lumps of life,
These four companions,—country-folk this time,
Not tainted by the unwholesome civic breath,
Much less the curse o' the Court! Mere striplings too,
Fit to do human nature justice still!   930
Surely when impudence in Guido's shape
Shall propose crime and proffer money's-worth
To these stout tall rough bright-eyed black-haired boys,
The blood shall bound in answer to each cheek
Before the indignant outcry break from lip!   935
Are these i' the mood to murder, hardly loosed
From healthy autumn-finish of ploughed glebe,
Grapes in the barrel, work at happy end,
And winter near with rest and Christmas play?
How greet they Guido with his final task—   940
(As if he but proposed " One vineyard more
" To dig, ere frost come, then relax indeed ! ")
" Anywhere, anyhow and anywhy,
" Murder me some three people, old and young,
" Ye never heard the names of,—and be paid   945
" So much ! "   And the whole four accede at once.
Demur?   Do cattle bidden march or halt?
Is it some lingering habit, old fond faith

I' the lord o' the land, instructs them,—birthright badge
Of feudal tenure claims its slaves again?   950
Not so at all, thou noble human heart !
All is done purely for the pay,—which, earned,
And not forthcoming at the instant, makes
Religion heresy, and the lord o' the land
Fit subject for a murder in his turn.   955
The patron with cut throat and rifled purse,
Deposited i' the roadside-ditch, his due,
Nought hinders each good fellow trudging home,
The heavier by a piece or two in poke,
And so with new zest to the common life,   960
Mattock and spade, plough-tail and waggon-shaft,
Till some such other piece of luck betide,
Who knows?   Since this is a mere start in life,
And none of them exceeds the twentieth year.
Nay, more i' the background yet?   Unnoticed forms
Claim to be classed, subordinately vile?   966
Complacent lookers-on that laugh,—perchance
Shake head as their.friend's horse-play grows too rough
With the mere child he manages amiss—
But would not interfere and make bad worse   970
For twice the fractious tears and prayers : thou know'st
Civility better, Marzi-Medici,
Governor for thy kinsman the Granduke !
Fit representative of law, man's lamp

I' the magistrate's grasp full-flare, no rushlight-end   975
Sputtering 'twixt thumb and finger of the priest!
Whose answer to the couple's cry for help
Is a threat,—whose remedy of Pompilia's wrong,
A shrug o' the shoulder, and facetious word
Or wink, traditional with Tuscan wits,   980
To Guido in the doorway.   Laud to law!
The wife is pushed back to the husband, he
Who knows how these home-squabblings persecute
People who have the public good to mind,
And work best with a silence in the court!   985

Ah, but I save my word at least for thee,
Archbishop, who art under, i' the Church,
As I am under God,—thou, chosen by both
To do the shepherd's office, feed the sheep—
How of this lamb that panted at thy foot   990
While the wolf pressed on her within crook's reach?
Wast thou the hireling that did turn and flee?
With thee at least anon the little word!

Such denizens o' the cave now cluster round
And heat the furnace sevenfold: time indeed   995
A bolt from heaven should cleave roof and clear place,
Transfix and show the world, suspiring flame,
The main offender, scar and brand the rest

Hurrying, each miscreant to his hole : then flood
And purify the scene with outside day—   1000
Which yet, in the absolutest drench of dark,
Ne'er wants a witness, some stray beauty-beam
To the despair of hell.

First of the first,
Such I pronounce Pompilia, then as now   1005
Perfect in whiteness : stoop thou down, my child,
Give one good moment to the poor old Pope
Heart-sick at having all his world to blame—
Let me look at thee in the flesh as erst,
Let me enjoy the old clean linen garb,   1010
Not the new splendid vesture !   Armed and crowned,
Would Michael, yonder, be, nor crowned nor armed,
The less pre-eminent angel ?   Everywhere
I see in the world the intellect of man,
That sword, the energy his subtle spear,   1015
The knowledge which defends him like a shield—
Everywhere ; but they make not up, I think,
The marvel of a soul like thine, earth's flower
She holds up to the softened gaze of God !
It was not given Pompilia to know much,   1020
Speak much, to write a book, to move mankind,
Be memorized by who records my time.
Yet if in purity and patience, if

In faith held fast despite the plucking fiend,
Safe like the signet stone with the new name   1025
That saints are known by,—if in right returned
For wrong, most pardon for worst injury,
If there be any virtue, any praise,—
Then will this woman-child have proved—who knows?—
Just the one prize vouchsafed unworthy me,   1030
Seven years a gardener of the untoward ground,
I till,—this earth, my sweat and blood manure
All the long day that barrenly grows dusk :
At least one blossom makes me proud at eve
Born 'mid the briers of my enclosure ! Still   1035
(Oh, here as elsewhere, nothingness of man !)
Those be the plants, imbedded yonder South
To mellow in the morning, those made fat
By the master's eye, that yield such timid leaf,
Uncertain bud, as product of his pains !   1040
While—see how this mere chance-sown cleft-nursed seed
That sprang up by the wayside 'neath the foot
Of the enemy, this breaks all into blaze,
Spreads itself, one wide glory of desire
To incorporate the whole great sun it loves   1045
From the inch-height whence it looks and longs! My
    flower,
My rose, I gather for the breast of God,
This I praise most in thee, where all I praise,

That having been obedient to the end
According to the light allotted, law   1050
Prescribed thy life, still tried, still standing test,—
Dutiful to the foolish parents first,
Submissive next to the bad husband,—nay,
Tolerant of those meaner miserable
That did his hests, eked out the dole of pain,— 1055
Thou, patient thus, couldst rise from law to law,
The old to the new, promoted at one cry
O' the trump of God to the new service, not
To longer bear, but henceforth fight, be found
Sublime in new impatience with the foe !   1060
Endure man and obey God : plant firm foot
On neck of man, tread man into the hell
Meet for him, and obey God all the more !
Oh child that didst despise thy life so much
When it seemed only thine to keep or lose,   1065
How the fine ear felt fall the first low word
" Value life, and preserve life for My sake ! "
Thou didst . . . how shall I say ? . . . receive so long
The standing ordinance of God on earth,
What wonder if the novel claim had clashed   1070
With old requirement, seemed to supersede
Too much the customary law ?   But, brave,
Thou at first prompting of what I call God,
And fools call Nature, didst hear, comprehend,

Accept the obligation laid on thee,   1075
Mother elect, to save the unborn child,
As brute and bird do, reptile and the fly,
Ay and, I nothing doubt, even tree, shrub, plant
And flower o' the field, all in a common pact
To worthily defend the trust of trusts,   1080
Life from the Ever Living:—didst resist—
Anticipate the office that is mine—
And with his own sword stay the upraised arm,
The endeavour of the wicked, and defend
Him who,—again in my default,—was there   1085
For visible providence : one less true than thou
To touch, i' the past, less practised in the right,
Approved less far in all docility
To all instruction,—how had such an one
Made scruple " Is this motion a decree ? "   1090
It was authentic to the experienced ear   .
O' the good and faithful servant.   Go past me
And get thy praise,—and be not far to seek
Presently when I follow if I may !

And surely not so very much apart   1095
Need I place thee, my warrior-priest,—in whom
What if I gain the other rose, the gold,
We grave to imitate God's miracle,
Greet monarchs with, good rose in its degree ?

Irregular noble'scapegrace—son the same!   1100
Faulty—and peradventure ours the fault
Who still misteach, mislead, throw hook and line,
Thinking to land leviathan forsooth,
Tame the scaled neck, play with him as a bird,
And bind him for our maidens! Better bear   1105
The King of Pride go wantoning awhile,
Unplagued by cord in nose and thorn in jaw,
Through deep to deep, followed by all that shine,
Churning the blackness hoary: He who made
The comely terror, He shall make the sword   1110
To match that piece of netherstone his heart,
Ay, nor miss praise thereby; who else shut fire
I' the stone, to leap from mouth at sword's first stroke,
In lamps of love and faith, the chivalry
That dares the right and disregards alike   1115
The yea and nay o' the world? Self-sacrifice,—
What if an idol took it? Ask the Church
Why she was wont to turn each Venus here,—
Poor Rome perversely lingered round, despite
Instruction, for the sake of purblind love,—   1120
Into Madonna's shape, and waste no whit
Of aught so rare on earth as gratitude!
All this sweet savour was not ours but thine,
Nard of the rock, a natural wealth we name
Incense, and treasure up as food for saints,   1125

When flung to us—whose function was to give
Not find the costly perfume.   Do I smile?
Nay, Caponsacchi, much I find amiss,
Blameworthy, punishable in this freak
Of thine, this youth prolonged, though age was ripe,
This masquerade in sober day, with change   1131
Of motley too,—now hypocrite's disguise,
Now fool's-costume : which lie was least like truth,
Which the ungainlier, more discordant garb
With that symmetric soul inside my son,   1135
The churchman's or the worldling's,—let him judge,
Our adversary who enjoys the task !
I rather chronicle the healthy rage,—
When the first moan broke from the martyr-maid
At that uncaging of the beasts,—made bare   1140
My athlete on the instant, gave such good
Great undisguised leap over post and pale
Right into the mid-cirque, free fighting-place.
There may have been rash stripping—every rag
Went to the winds,—infringement manifold   1145
Of laws prescribed pudicity, I fear,
In this impulsive and prompt self-display !
Ever such tax comes of the foolish youth ;
Men mulct the wiser manhood, and suspect
No veritable star swims out of cloud.   1150
Bear thou such imputation, undergo

The penalty I nowise dare relax,—
Conventional chastisement and rebuke.
But for the outcome, the brave starry birth
Conciliating earth with all that cloud,   1155
Thank heaven as I do!   Ay, such championship
Of God at first blush, such prompt cheery thud
Of glove on ground that answers ringingly
The challenge of the false knight,—watch we long
And wait we vainly for its gallant like   1160
From those appointed to the service, sworn
His body-guard with pay and privilege—
White-cinct, because in white walks sanctity,
Red-socked, how else proclaim fine scorn of flesh,
Unchariness of blood when blood faith begs !   1165
Where are the men-at-arms with cross on coat?
Aloof, bewraying their attire : whilst thou
In mask and motley, pledged to dance not fight,
Sprang'st forth the hero !   In thought, word and deed,
How throughout all thy warfare thou wast pure,   1170
I find it easy to believe : and if
At any fateful moment of the strange
Adventure, the strong passion of that strait,
Fear and surprise, may have revealed too much,—
As when a thundrous midnight, with black air   1175
That burns, rain-drops that blister, breaks a spell,
Draws out the excessive virtue of some sheathed

Shut unsuspected flower that hoards and hides
Immensity of sweetness,—so, perchance,
Might the surprise and fear release too much   1180
The perfect beauty of the body and soul
Thou savedst in thy passion for God's sake,
He who is Pity. Was the trial sore?
Temptation sharp? Thank God a second time!
Why comes temptation but for man to meet   1185
And master and make crouch beneath his foot,
And so be pedestaled in triumph? Pray
"Lead us into no such temptations, Lord!"
Yea, but, O Thou whose servants are the bold,
Lead such temptations by the head and hair,   1190
Reluctant dragons, up to who dares fight,
That so he may do battle and have praise!
Do I not see the praise?—that while thy mates
Bound to deserve i' the matter, prove at need
Unprofitable through the very pains   1195
We gave to train them well and start them fair,—
Are found too stiff, with standing ranked and ranged,
For onset in good earnest, too obtuse
Of ear, through iteration of command,
For catching quick the sense of the real cry,—   1200
Thou, whose sword-hand was used to strike the lute,
Whose sentry-station graced some wanton's gate,
Thou didst push forward and show mettle, shame

The laggards, and retrieve the day.   Well done!
Be glad thou hast let light into the world   1205
Through that irregular breach o' the boundary,—see
The same upon thy path and march assured,
Learning anew the use of soldiership,
Self-abnegation, freedom from all fear,
Loyalty to the life's end!   Ruminate,   1210
Deserve the initiatory spasm,--once more
Work, be unhappy but bear life, my son!

And troop you, somewhere 'twixt the best and worst,
Where crowd the indifferent product, all too poor
Makeshift, starved samples of humanity!   1215
Father and mother, huddle there and hide!
A gracious eye may find you!   Foul and fair,
Sadly mixed natures : self-indulgent,—yet
Self-sacrificing too : how the love soars,
How the craft, avarice, vanity and spite   1220
Sink again!   So they keep the middle course,
Slide into silly crime at unaware,
Slip back upon the stupid virtue, stay
Nowhere enough for being classed, I hope
And fear.   Accept the swift and rueful death,   1225
Taught, somewhat sternlier than is wont, what waits
The ambiguous creature,—how the one black tuft
Steadies the aim of the arrow just as well

As the wide faultless white on the bird's breast!
Nay, you were punished in the very part   1230
That looked most pure of speck,—'t was honest
    love
Betrayed you,—did love seem most worthy pains,
Challenge such purging, since ordained survive
When all the rest of you was done with?   Go!
Never again elude the choice of tints!   1235
White shall not neutralize the black, nor good
Compensate bad in man, absolve him so:
Life's business being just the terrible choice.

So do I see, pronounce on all and some
Grouped for my judgment now,—profess no doubt
While I pronounce: dark, difficult enough   1241
The human sphere, yet eyes grow sharp by use,
I find the truth, dispart the shine from shade,
As a mere man may, with no special touch
O' the lynx-gift in each ordinary orb: 1245
Nay, if the popular notion class me right,
One of well-nigh decayed intelligence,—
What of that?   Through hard labour and good will,
And habitude that gives a blind man sight
At the practised finger-ends of him, I do   1250
Discern, and dare decree in consequence,
Whatever prove the peril of mistake.

    x.   I

Whence, then, this quite new quick cold thrill,—cloud-
    like,
This keen dread creeping from a quarter scarce
Suspected in the skies I nightly scan?   1255
What slacks the tense nerve, saps the wound-up spring
Of the act that should and shall be, sends the mount
And mass o' the whole man's-strength,—conglobed so
    late—
Shudderingly into dust, a moment's work?
While I stand firm, go fearless, in this world,   1260
For this life recognize and arbitrate,   .
Touch and let stay, or else remove a thing,
Judge " This is right, this object out of place,"
Candle in hand that helps me and to spare,—
What if a voice deride me, " Perk and pry !   1265
" Brighten each nook with thine intelligence !
" Play the good householder, ply man and maid
" With tasks prolonged into the midnight, test
" Their work and nowise stint of the due wage
" Each worthy worker : but with gyves and whip   1270
" Pay thou misprision of a single point
" Plain to thy happy self who lift'st the light,
" Lament'st the darkling,—bold to all beneath !
" What if thyself adventure, now the place
" Is purged so well ?   Leave pavement and mount roof,
' Look round thee for the light of the upper sky,   1276

"The fire which lit thy fire which finds default
"In Guido Franceschini to his cost !
"What if, above in the domain of light,
"Thou miss the accustomed signs, remark eclipse ?
"Shalt thou still gaze on ground nor lift a lid,— 128ɪ
"Steady in thy superb prerogative,
"Thy inch of inkling,—nor once face the doubt
"I' the sphere above thee, darkness to be felt ?"

Yet my poor spark had for its source, the sun ; 1285
Thither I sent the great looks which compel
Light from its fount : all that I do and am
Comes from the truth, or seen or else surmised,
Remembered or divined, as mere man may :
I know just so, nor otherwise.   As I know, 1290
I speak,—what should I know, then, and how speak
Were there a wild mistake of eye or brain
As to recorded governance above ?
If my own breath, only, blew coal alight
I styled celestial and the morning-star ? 1295
I, who in this world act resolvedly,
Dispose of men, their bodies and their souls,
As they acknowledge or gainsay the light
I show them,—shall I too lack courage ?—leave
I, too, the post of me, like those I blame ? 1300
Refuse, with kindred inconsistency,

To grapple danger whereby souls grow strong?
I am near the end; but still not at the end;
All to the very end is trial in life:
At this stage is the trial of my soul   1305
Danger to face, or danger to refuse?
Shall I dare try the doubt now, or not dare?

O Thou,—as represented here to me
In such conception as my soul allows,—
Under Thy measureless, my atom width!—   1310
Man's mind, what is it but a convex glass
Wherein are gathered all the scattered points
Picked out of the immensity of sky,
To re-unite there, be our heaven for earth,
Our known unknown, our God revealed to man?
Existent somewhere, somehow, as a whole;   1316
Here, as a whole proportioned to our sense,—
There, (which is nowhere, speech must babble thus!)
In the absolute immensity, the whole
Appreciable solely by Thyself,—   1320
Here, by the little mind of man, reduced
To littleness that suits his faculty,
In the degree appreciable too;
Between Thee and ourselves—nay even, again,
Below us, to the extreme of the minute,   1325
Appreciable by how many and what diverse

Modes of the life Thou madest be ! (why live
Except for love,—how love unless they know ?)
Each of them, only filling to the edge,
Insect or angel, his just length and breadth, 1330
Due facet of reflection,—full, no less,
Angel or insect, as Thou framedst things.
I it is who have been appointed here
To represent Thee, in my turn, on earth,
Just as, if new philosophy know aught, 1335
This one earth, out of all the multitude
Of peopled worlds, as stars are now supposed,—
Was chosen, and no sun-star of the swarm,
For stage and scene of Thy transcendent act
Beside which even the creation fades 1340
Into a puny exercise of power.
Choice of the world, choice of the thing I am,
Both emanate alike from Thy dread play
Of operation outside this our sphere
Where things are classed and counted small or great,—
Incomprehensibly the choice is Thine ! 1346
I therefore bow my head and take Thy place.
There is, beside the works, a tale of Thee
In the world's mouth, which I find credible :
I love it with my heart : unsatisfied, 1350
I try it with my reason, nor discept
From any point I probe and pronounce sound.

Mind is not matter nor from matter, but
Above,—leave matter then, proceed with mind!
Man's be the mind recognized at the height,—   1355
Leave the inferior minds and look at man!
Is he the strong, intelligent and good
Up to his own conceivable height?   Nowise.
Enough o' the low,—soar the conceivable height,
Find cause to match the effect in evidence,   1360
The work i'' the world, not man's but God's; leave
    man!
Conjecture of the worker by the work:
Is there strength there?—enough: intelligence?
Ample: but goodness in a like degree?
Not to the human eye in the present state,   1365
An isoscele deficient in the base.
What lacks, then, of perfection fit for God
But just the instance which this tale supplies
Of love without a limit?   So is strength,
So is intelligence; let love be so,   1370
Unlimited in its self-sacrifice,
Then is the tale true and God shows complete.
Beyond the tale, I reach into the dark,
Feel what I cannot see, and still faith stands:
I can believe this dread machinery   1375
Of sin and sorrow, would confound me else,
Devised,—all pain, at most expenditure

Of pain by Who devised pain,—to evolve,
By new machinery in counterpart,
The moral qualities of man—how else ?—   1380
To make him love in turn and be beloved,
Creative and self-sacrificing too,
And thus eventually God-like, (ay,
" I have said ye are Gods,"—shall it be said for nought ?)
Enable man to wring, from out all pain,   1385
All pleasure for a common heritage
To all eternity : this may be surmised,
The other is revealed,—whether a fact,
Absolute, abstract, independent truth,
Historic, not reduced to suit man's mind,—   1390
Or only truth reverberate, changed, made pass
A spectrum, into mind, the narrow eye,—
The same and not the same, else unconceived—
Though quite conceivable to the next grade
Above it in intelligence,—as truth   1395
Easy to man were blindness to the beast
By parity of procedure,—the same truth
In a new form, but changed in either case :
What matter so intelligence be filled ?
To a child, the sea is angry, for it roars :   1400
Frost bites, else why the tooth-like fret on face?
Man makes acoustics deal with the sea's wrath,
Explains the choppy cheek by chymic law,—

To man and child remains the same effect
On drum of ear and root of nose, change cause   1405
Never so thoroughly : so my heart be struck,
What care I,—by God's gloved hand or the bare ?
Nor do I much perplex me with aught hard,
Dubious in the transmitting of the tale,—
No, nor with certain riddles set to solve.   1410
This life is training and a passage ; pass,—
Still, we march over some flat obstacle
We made give way before us ; solid truth
In front of it, what motion for the world ?
The moral sense grows but by exercise.   1415
'T is even as man grew probatively
Initiated in Godship, set to make
A fairer moral world than this he finds,
Guess now what shall be known hereafter.   Deal
Thus with the present problem : as we see,   1420
A faultless creature is destroyed, and sin
Has had its way i' the world where God should rule.
Ay, but for this irrelevant circumstance
Of inquisition after blood, we see
Pompilia lost and Guido saved : how long ?   1425
For his whole life : how much is that whole life ?
We are not babes, but know the minute's worth,
And feel that life is large and the world small,
So, wait till life have passed from out the world.

Neither does this astonish at the end,   1430
That whereas I can so receive and trust,
Other men, made with hearts and souls the same,
Reject and disbelieve,—subordinate
The future to the present,—sin, nor fear.
This I refer still to the foremost fact,   1435
Life is probation and the earth no goal
But starting-point of man : compel him strive,
Which means, in man, as good as reach the goal,—
Why institute that race, his life, at all?
But this does overwhelm me with surprise,   1440
Touch me to terror,—not that faith, the pearl,
Should be let lie by fishers wanting food,—
Nor, seen and handled by a certain few
Critical and contemptuous, straight consigned
To shore and shingle for the pebble it proves,—   1445
But that, when haply found and known and named
By the residue made rich for evermore,
These,—that these favoured ones, should in a trice
Turn, and with double zest go dredge for whelks,
Mud-worms that make the savoury soup !   Enough 1450
O' the disbelievers, see the faithful few !
How do the Christians here deport them, keep
Their robes of white unspotted by the world?
What is this Aretine Archbishop, this
Man under me as I am under God,   1455

This champion of the faith, I armed and decked,
Pushed forward, put upon a pinnacle,
To show the enemy his victor,—see !
What 's the best fighting when the couple close ?
Pompilia cries, " Protect me from the wolf ! "   1460
He—" No, thy Guido is rough, heady, strong,
" Dangerous to disquiet : let him bide !
" He needs some bone to mumble, help amuse
" The darkness of his den with : so, the fawn
" Which limps up bleeding to my foot and lies,   1465
" —Come to me, daughter !—thus I throw him back ! "
Have we misjudged here, over-armed our knight,
Given gold and silk where plain hard steel serves best,
Enfeebled whom we sought to fortify,
Made an archbishop and undone a saint?   1470
Well, then, descend these heights, this pride of life,
Sit in the ashes with a barefoot monk
Who long ago stamped out the worldly sparks,
By fasting, watching, stone cell and wire scourge,
—No such indulgence as unknits the strength—   1475
These breed the tight nerve and tough cuticle,
And the world's praise or blame runs rillet-wise
Off the broad back and brawny breast, we know !
He meets the first cold sprinkle of the world,
And shudders to the marrow. " Save this child?   1480
" Oh, my superiors, oh, the Archbishop's self !

" Who was it dared lay hand upon the ark
" His betters saw fall nor put finger forth ?
" Great ones could help yet help not : why should small ?
" I break my promise : let her break her heart ! "   1485
These are the Christians not the worldlings, not
The sceptics, who thus battle for the faith !
If foolish virgins disobey and sleep,
What wonder ?   But, this time, the wise that watch,
Sell lamps and buy lutes, exchange oil for wine,   1490
The mystic Spouse betrays the Bridegroom here.
To our last resource, then !   Since all flesh is weak,
Bind weaknesses together, we get strength :
The individual weighed, found wanting, try
Some institution, honest artifice   1495
Whereby the units grow compact and firm !
Each props the other, and so stand is made
By our embodied cowards that grow brave.
The Monastery called of Convertites,
Meant to help women because these helped Christ,—
A thing existent only while it acts,   1501
Does as designed, else a nonentity,—
For what is an idea unrealized ?—
Pompilia is consigned to these for help.
They do help : they are prompt to testify   1505
To her pure life and saintly dying days.
She dies, and lo, who seemed so poor, proves rich.

What does the body that lives through helpfulness
To women for Christ's sake?   The kiss turns bite,
The dove's note changes to the crow's cry: judge! 1510
" Seeing that this our Convent claims of right
" What goods belong to those we succour, be
" The same proved women of dishonest life,—
" And seeing that this Trial made appear
" Pompilia was in such predicament,—   1515
" The Convent hereupon pretends to said
" Succession of Pompilia, issues writ,
" And takes possession by the Fisc's advice."
Such is their attestation to the cause
Of Christ, who had one saint at least, they hoped: 1520
But, is a title-deed to filch, a corpse
To slander, and an infant-heir to cheat?
Christ must give up his gains then!   They unsay
All the fine speeches,—who was saint is whore.
Why, scripture yields no parallel for this!   1525
The soldiers only threw dice for Christ's coat;
We want another legend of the Twelve
Disputing if it was Christ's coat at all,
Claiming as prize the woof of price—for why?
The Master was a thief, purloined the same,   1530
Or paid for it out of the common bag!
Can it be this is end and outcome, all
I take with me to show as stewardship's fruit,

The best yield of the latest time, this year
The seventeen-hundredth since God died for man? 1535
Is such effect proportionate to cause?
And still the terror keeps on the increase
When I perceive . . . how can I blink the fact?
That the fault, the obduracy to good,
Lies not with the impracticable stuff   1540
Whence man is made, his very nature's fault,
As if it were of ice the moon may gild
Not melt, or stone 't was meant the sun should warm
Not make bear flowers,—nor ice nor stone to blame :
But it can melt, that ice, can bloom, that stone,   1545
Impassible to rule of day and night !
This terrifies me, thus compelled perceive,
Whatever love and faith we looked should spring
At advent of the authoritative star,
Which yet lie sluggish, curdled at the source,—   1550
These have leapt forth profusely in old time,
These still respond with promptitude to-day,
At challenge of—what unacknowledged powers
O' the air, what uncommissioned meteors, warmth
By law, and light by rule should supersede?   1555
For see this priest, this Caponsacchi, stung
At the first summons,—" Help for honour's sake,
" Play the man, pity the oppressed !"—no pause,
How does he lay about him in the midst,

Strike any foe, right wrong at any risk,   1560
All blindness, bravery and obedience !—blind ?
Ay, as a man would be inside the sun,
Delirious with the plenitude of light
Should interfuse him to the finger-ends—
Let him rush straight, and how shall he go wrong ? 1565
Where are the Christians in their panoply ?
·The loins we girt about with truth, the breasts
Righteousness plated round, the shield of faith,
The helmet of salvation, and that sword
O' the Spirit, even the word of God,—where these ? 1570
Slunk into corners !   Oh, I hear at once
Hubbub of protestation !   " What, we monks
" We friars, of such an order, such a rule,
" Have not we fought, bled, left our martyr-mark
" At every point along the boundary-line   1575
" 'Twixt true and false, religion and the world,
" Where this or the other dogma of our Church
" Called for defence ? "   And I, despite myself,
How can I but speak loud what truth speaks low,
" Or better than the best, or nothing serves !   1580
" What boots deed, I can cap and cover straight
·" With such another doughtiness to match,
" Done at an instinct of the natural man ? "
Immolate body, sacrifice soul too,—
Do not these publicans the same ?   Outstrip !   1585

Or else stop race you boast runs neck and neck,
You with the wings, they with the feet,—for shame!
Oh, I remark your diligence and zeal!
Five years long, now, rounds faith into my ears,
" Help thou, or Christendom is done to death !" 1590
Five years since, in the Province of To-kien,
Which is in China as some people know,
Maigrot, my Vicar Apostolic there,
Having a great qualm, issues a decree.
Alack, the converts use as God's name, not   1595
Tien-chu but plain *Tien* or else mere *Shang-ti,*
As Jesuits please to fancy politic,
. While, say Dominicans, it calls down fire,—
For *Tien* means heaven, and *Shang-ti,* supreme prince,
While *Tien-chu* means the lord of heaven : all cry,
" There is no business urgent for despatch   1601
" As that thou send a legate, specially
" Cardinal Tournon, straight to Pekin, there
" To settle and compose the difference !"
So have I seen a potentate all fume   1605
For some infringement of his realm's just right,
Some menace to a mud-built straw-thatched farm
O' the frontier ; while inside the mainland lie,
Quite undisputed-for in solitude,
Whole cities plague may waste or famine sap: 1610
What if the sun crumble, the sands encroach,

While he looks on sublimely at his ease?
How does their ruin touch the empire's bound?

And is this little all that was to be?
Where is the gloriously-decisive change,   1615
Metamorphosis the immeasurable
Of human clay to divine gold, we looked
Should, in some poor sort, justify its price?
Had an adept of the mere Rosy Cross
Spent his life to consummate the Great Work,   1620
Would not we start to see the stuff it touched
Yield not a grain more than the vulgar got
By the old smelting-process years ago?
If this were sad to see in just the sage
Who should profess so much, perform no more,   1625
What is it when suspected in that Power
Who undertook to make and made the world,
Devised and did effect man, body and soul,
Ordained salvation for them both, and yet . . .
Well, is the thing we see, salvation?   1630
                              I
Put no such dreadful question to myself,
Within whose circle of experience burns
The central truth, Power, Wisdom, Goodness,—God:
I must outlive a thing ere know it dead: 1635
When I outlive the faith there is a sun,

When I lie, ashes to the very soul,—
Someone, not I, must wail above the heap,
" He died in dark whence never morn arose."
While I see day succeed the deepest night—   1640
How can I speak but as I know?—my speech
Must be, throughout the darkness, "It will end:
" The light that did burn, will burn!" Clouds obscure—
But for which obscuration all were bright?
Too hastily concluded! Sun-suffused,   1645
A cloud may soothe the eye made blind by blaze,—
Better the very clarity of heaven:
The soft streaks are the beautiful and dear.
What but the weakness in a faith supplies
The incentive to humanity, no strength   1650
Absolute, irresistible, comports?
How can man love but what he yearns to help?
And that which men think weakness within strength,
But angels know for strength and stronger yet—
What were it else but the first things made new,   1655
But repetition of the miracle,
The divine instance of self-sacrifice
That never ends and aye begins for man?
So, never I miss footing in the maze,
No,—I have light nor fear the dark at all.   1660

But are mankind not real, who pace outside
   X.   K

My petty circle, world that 's measured me ?
And when they stumble even as I stand,
Have I a right to stop ear when they cry,
As they were phantoms who took clouds for crags,   1665
Tripped and fell, where man's march might safely move?
Beside, the cry is other than a ghost's,
When out of the old time there pleads some bard,
Philosopher, or both, and—whispers not,
But words it boldly.   "The inward work and worth   1670
" Of any mind, what other mind may judge
" Save God who only knows the thing He made,
" The veritable service He exacts?
" It is the outward product men appraise.
" Behold, an engine hoists a tower aloft :   1675
" ' I looked that it should move the mountàin too ! '
" Or else ' Had just a turret toppled down,
" ' Success enough ! '—may say the Machinist
" Who knows what less or more result might be :
" But we, who see that done we cannot do,   1680
" ' A feat beyond man's force,' we men must say.
" Regard me and that shake I gave the world !
" I was born, not so long before Christ's birth
" As Christ's birth haply did precede thy day,—
" But many a watch before the star of dawn :   1685
" Therefore I lived,—it is thy creed affirms,
" Pope Innocent, who art to answer me !—

" Under conditions, nowise to escape,
" Whereby salvation was impossible.
" Each impulse to achieve the good and fair,   1690
" Each aspiration to the pure and true,
" Being without a warrant or an aim,
" Was just as sterile a felicity
" As if the insect, born to spend his life
" Soaring his circles, stopped them to describe   1695
" (Painfully motionless in the mid-air)
" Some word of weighty counsel for man's sake,
" Some 'Know thyself' or 'Take the golden mean!'
" —Forwent his happy dance and the glad ray,
" Died half an hour the sooner and was dust.   1700
" I, born to perish like the brutes, or worse,
" Why not live brutishly, obey brutes' law?
" But I, of body as of soul complete,
" A gymnast at the games, philosopher
" I' the schools, who painted, and made music,—all
" Glories that met upon the tragic stage   1706
" When the Third Poet's tread surprised the Two,—
" Whose lot fell in a land where life was great
" And sense went free and beauty lay profuse,
" I, untouched by one adverse circumstance,   1710
" Adopted virtue as my rule of life,
" Waived all reward, loved but for loving's sake,
" And, what my heart taught me, I taught the world,

K 2

" And have been teaching now two thousand years.
" Witness my work,—plays that should please, forsooth!
" ' They might please, they may displease, they shall
      teach,   1716
" ' For truth's sake,' so I said, and did, and do.
" Five hundred years ere Paul spoke, Felix heard,—
" How much of temperance and righteousness,
" Judgment to come, did I find reason for,   1720
" Corroborate with my strong style that spared
" No sin, nor swerved the more from branding brow
" Because the sinner was called Zeus and God?
" How nearly did I guess at that Paul knew?
" How closely come, in what I represent   1725
" As duty, to his doctrine yet a blank?
" And as that limner not untruly limns
" Who draws an object round or square, which square
" Or round seems to the unassisted eye,
" Though Galileo's tube display the same   1730
" Oval or oblong,—so, who controverts
" I rendered rightly what proves wrongly wrought
" Beside Paul's picture?   Mine was true for me.
" I saw that there are, first and above all,
" The hidden forces, blind necessities,   1735
" Named Nature, but the thing's self unconceived :
" Then follow,—how dependent upon these,
" We know not, how imposed above ourselves,

" We well know,—what I name the gods, a power
" Various or one : for great and strong and good
" Is there, and little, weak and bad there too,   1741
" Wisdom and folly : say, these make no God,—
" What is it else that rules outside man's self?
" A fact then,—always, to the naked eye,—
" And so, the one revealment possible   1745
" Of what were unimagined else by man.
" Therefore, what gods do, man may criticize,
"Applaud, condemn,—how should he fear the truth?—
" But likewise have in awe because of power,
" Venerate for the main munificence,   1750
" And give the doubtful deed its due excuse
" From the acknowledged creature of a day
" To the Eternal and Divine.   Thus, bold
" Yet self-mistrusting, should man bear himself,
" Most assured on what now concerns him most—
" The law of his own life, the path he prints,—   1756
" Which law is virtue and not vice, I say,—
" And least inquisitive where search least skills,
" I' the nature we best give the clouds to keep.
" What could I paint beyond a scheme like this   1760
" Out of the fragmentary truths where light
" Lay fitful in a tenebrific time?
" You have the sunrise now, joins truth to truth,
" Shoots life and substance into death and void ;

" Themselves compose the whole we made before :
" The forces and necessity grow God,—   1766
" The beings so contrarious that seemed gods,
" Prove just His operation manifold
" And multiform, translated, as must be,
" Into intelligible shape so far   1770
" As suits our sense and sets us free to feel.
" What if I let a child think, childhood-long,
" That lightning, I would have him spare his eye,
" Is a real arrow shot at naked orb?   1774
" The man knows more, but shuts his lids the same :
" Lightning's cause comprehends nor man nor child.
" Why then, my scheme, your better knowledge broke,
" Presently re-adjusts itself, the small
" Proportioned largelier, parts and whole named new :
" So much, no more two thousand years have done !
" Pope, dost thou dare pretend to punish me,   1781
" For not descrying sunshine at midnight,
" Me who crept all-fours, found my way so far—
" While thou rewardest teachers of the truth,   1784
" Who miss the plain way in the blaze of noon,—
" Though just a word from that strong style of mine,
" Grasped honestly in hand as guiding-staff,
" Had pricked them a sure path across the bog,
" That mire of cowardice and slush of lies
" Wherein I find them wallow in wide day ! "   1790

How should I answer this Euripides?
Paul,—'t is a legend,—answered Seneca,
But that was in the day-spring; noon is now:
We have got too familiar with the light.　　1794
Shall I wish back once more that thrill of dawn?
When the whole truth-touched man burned up, one fire?
—Assured the trial, fiery, fierce, but fleet,
Would, from his little heap of ashes, lend
Wings to that conflagration of the world
Which Christ awaits ere He makes all things new:
So should the frail become the perfect, rapt　　1801
From glory of pain to glory of joy ; and so,
Even in the end,—the act renouncing earth,
Lands, houses, husbands, wives and children here,—
Begin that other act which finds all, lost,　　1805
Regained, in this time even, a hundredfold,
And, in the next time, feels the finite love
Blent and embalmed with the eternal life.
So does the sun ghastlily seem to sink
In those north parts, lean all but out of life,　　1810
Desist a dread mere breathing-stop, then slow
Re-assert day, begin the endless rise.
Was this too easy for our after-stage?
Was such a lighting-up of faith, in life,
Only allowed initiate, set man's step　　1815
In the true way by help of the great glow?

A way wherein it is ordained he walk,
Bearing to see the light from heaven still more
And more encroached on by the light of earth,
Tentatives earth puts forth to rival heaven,   1820
Earthly incitements that mankind serve God
For man's sole sake, not God's and therefore man's.
Till at last, who distinguishes the sun
From a mere Druid fire on a far mount?
More praise to him who with his subtle prism   1825
Shall decompose both beams and name the true.
In such sense, who is last proves first indeed ·
For how could saints and martyrs fail see truth
Streak the night's blackness?   Who is faithful now?
Who untwists heaven's white from the yellow flare
O' the world's gross torch, without night's foil that helped
Produce the Christian act so possible   1832
When in the way stood Nero's cross and stake,—
So hard now when the world smiles " Right and wise !
" Faith points the politic, the thrifty way,   1835
" Will make who plods it in the end returns
" Beyond mere fool's-sport and improvidence.
" We fools dance thro' the cornfield of this life,
" Pluck ears to left and right and swallow raw,
" —Nay, tread, at pleasure, a sheaf underfoot,   1840
" To get the better at some poppy-flower,—
" Well aware we shall have so much less wheat

" In the eventual harvest : you meantime
" Waste not a spike,—the richlier will you reap !
" What then?   There will be always garnered meal
" Sufficient for our comfortable loaf,   1846
" While you enjoy the undiminished sack ! "
Is it not this ignoble confidence,
Cowardly hardihood, that dulls and damps,
Makes the old heroism impossible?   1850

Unless . . . what whispers me of times to come?
What if it be the mission of that age
My death will usher into life, to shake
This torpor of assurance from our creed,
Re-introduce the doubt discarded, bring   1855
That formidable danger back, we drove
Long ago to the distance and the dark?
No wild beast now prowls round the infant camp :
We have built wall and sleep in city safe :
But if some earthquake try the towers that laugh
To think they once saw lions rule outside,   1861
And man stand out again, pale, resolute,
Prepared to die,—which means, alive at last?
As we broke up that old faith of the world,
Have we, next age, to break up this the new—   1865
Faith, in the thing, grown faith in the report—
Whence need to bravely disbelieve report

Through increased faith i' the thing reports belie?
Must we deny,—do they, these Molinists,
At peril of their body and their soul,—   1870
Recognized truths, obedient to some truth
Unrecognized yet, but perceptible?—
Correct the portrait by the living face,
Man's God, by God's God in the mind of man?
Then, for the few that rise to the new height,   1875
The many that must sink to the old depth,
The multitude found fall away!   A few,
E'en ere new law speak clear, may keep the old,
Preserve the Christian level, call good good
And evil evil, (even though razed and blank   1880
The old titles,) helped by custom, habitude,
And all else they mistake for finer sense
O' the fact that reason warrants,—as before,
They hope perhaps, fear not impossibly.
At least some one Pompilia left the world   1885
Will say " I know the right place by foot's feel,
" I took it and tread firm there ; wherefore change?"
But what a multitude will surely fall
Quite through the crumbling truth, late subjacent,
Sink to the next discoverable base,   1890
Rest upon human nature, settle there
On what is firm, the lust and pride of life !
A mass of men, whose very souls even now

Seem to need re-creating,—so they slink
Worm-like into the mud, light now lays bare,—   1895
Whose future we dispose of with shut eyes
And whisper—" They are grafted, barren twigs,
" Into the living stock of Christ : may bear
" One day, till when they lie death-like, not dead,"—
Those who with all the aid of Christ succumb,   1900
How, without Christ, shall they, unaided, sink?
Whither but to this gulf before my eyes ?
Do not we end, the century and I ?
The impatient antimasque treads close on kibe
O' the very masque's self it will mock,—on me,   1905
Last lingering personage, the impatient mime
Pushes already,—will I block the way?
Will my slow trail of garments ne'er leave space
For pantaloon, sock, plume and castanet?
Here comes the first experimentalist   1910
In the new order of things,—he plays a priest ;
Does he take inspiration from the Church,
Directly make her rule his law of life?
Not he : his own mere impulse guides the man—
Happily sometimes, since ourselves allow   1915
He has danced, in gaiety of heart, i' the main
The right step through the maze we bade him foot.
But if his heart had prompted him break loose
And mar the measure?   Why, we must submit,

And thank the chance that brought him safe so far.
Will he repeat the prodigy?   Perhaps.   1921
Can he teach others how to quit themselves,
Show why this step was right while that were wrong?
How should he?   "Ask your hearts as I asked mine,
" And get discreetly through the morrice too;   1925
" If your hearts misdirect you,—quit the stage,
" And make amends,—be there amends to make!"
Such is, for the Augustin that was once,
This Canon Caponsacchi we see now.
" But my heart answers to another tune,"   1930
Puts in the Abate, second in the suite,
" I have my taste too, and tread no such step!
" You choose the glorious life, and may, for me!
" I like the lowest of life's appetites,—
" So you judge,—but the very truth of joy   1935
" To my own apprehension which decides.
" Call me knave and you get yourself called fool!
" I live for greed, ambition, lust, revenge;
" Attain these ends by force, guile: hypocrite,
" To-day, perchance to-morrow recognized   194?
" The rational man, the type of common sense."
There's Loyola adapted to our time!
Under such guidance Guido plays his part,
He also influencing in the due turn
These last clods where I track intelligence   194

By any glimmer, these four at his beck
Ready to murder any, and, at their own,
As ready to murder him,—such make the world !
And, first effect of the new cause of things,
There they lie also duly,—the old pair   1950
Of the weak head and not so wicked heart,
With the one Christian mother, wife and girl,
—Which three gifts seem to make an angel up,—
The world's first foot o' the dance is on their heads !
Still, I stand here, not off the stage though close 1955
On the exit : and my last act, as my first,
I owe the scene, and Him who armed me thus
With Paul's sword as with Peter's key.   I smite
With my whole strength once more, ere end my part,
Ending, so far as man may, this offence.   1960
And when I raise my arm, who plucks my sleeve?
Who stops me in the righteous function,—foe
Or friend?   Oh, still as ever, friends are they
Who, in the interest of outraged truth
Deprecate such rough handling of a lie !   1965
The facts being proved and incontestable,
What is the last word I must listen to?
Perchance—"Spare yet a term this barren stock
" We pray thee dig about and dung and dress
" Till he repent and bring forth fruit even yet ! " 1970
Perchance—" So poor and swift a punishment

" Shall throw him out of life with all that sin :
" Let mercy rather pile up pain on pain
" Till the flesh expiate what the soul pays else ! "
Nowise !   Remonstrants on each side commence
Instructing, there 's a new tribunal now   197
Higher than God's—the educated man's !
Nice sense of honour in the human breast
Supersedes here the old coarse oracle—
Confirming none the less a point or so   198
Wherein blind predecessors worked aright
By rule of thumb : as when Christ said,—when, where
Enough, I find it pleaded in a place,—
" All other wrongs done, patiently I take :
" But touch my honour and the case is changed !
" I feel the due resentment,—*nemini*   198
" *Honorem trado* is my quick retort."
Right of Him, just as if pronounced to-day !
Still, should the old authority be mute
Or doubtful or in speaking clash with new,   199
The younger takes permission to decide.
At last we have the instinct of the world
Ruling its household without tutelage :
And while the two laws, human and divine,
Have busied finger with this tangled case,   199
In pushes the brisk junior, cuts the knot,
Pronounces for acquittal.   How it trips

Silverly o'er the tongue! " Remit the death!

" Forgive, . . . well, in the old way, if thou please,

" Decency and the relics of routine   2000

" Respected,—let the Count go free as air!

" Since he may plead a priest's immunity,—

" The minor orders help enough for that,

" With Farinacci's licence,—who decides

" That the mere implication of such man,   2005

" So privileged, in any cause, before

" Whatever Court except the Spiritual,

" Straight quashes law-procedure,—quash it, then!

" Remains a pretty loophole of escape

" Moreover, that, beside the patent fact   2010

" O' the law's allowance, there 's involvèd the weal

" O' the Popedom : a son's privilege at stake,

" Thou wilt pretend the Church's interest,

" Ignore all finer reasons to forgive!

" But herein lies the crowning cogency—   2015

" (Let thy friends teach thee while thou tellest beads)

" That in this case the spirit of culture speaks,

" Civilization is imperative.

" To her shall we remand all delicate points

" Henceforth, nor take irregular advice   2020

" O' the sly, as heretofore : she used to hint

" Remonstrances, when law was out of sorts

" Because a saucy tongue was put to rest,

" An eye that roved was cured of arrogance :
" But why be forced to mumble under breath   2025
" What soon shall be acknowledged as plain fact,
" Outspoken, say, in thy successor's time?
" Methinks we see the golden age return !
" Civilization and the Emperor
" Succeed to Christianity and Pope.   2030
" One Emperor then, as one Pope now : meanwhile,
" Anticipate a little ! We tell thee 'Take
" ' Guido's life, sapped society shall crash,
" ' Whereof the main prop was, is, and shall be
" ' —Supremacy of husband over wife !'   2035
" Does the man rule i' the house, and may his mate
" Because of any plea dispute the same?
" Oh, pleas of all sorts shall abound, be sure,
" One but allowed validity,—for, harsh
" And savage, for, inept and silly-sooth,   · 2040
" For, this and that, will the ingenious sex
" Demonstrate the best master e'er graced slave :
" And there 's but one short way to end the coil,—
" Acknowledge right and reason steadily
" I' the man and master : then the wife submits 2045
" To plain truth broadly stated.   Does the time
" Advise we shift—a pillar? nay, a stake
" Out of its place i' the social tenement?
" One touch may send a shudder through the heap

" And bring it toppling on our children's heads ! 2050
" Moreover, if ours breed a qualm in thee,
" Give thine own better feeling play for once !
" Thou, whose own life winks o'er the socket-edge,
"Wouldst thou it went out in such ugly snuff
" As dooming sons dead, e'en though justice prompt?
" Why, on a certain feast, Barabbas' self   2056
" Was set free, not to cloud the general cheer:
" Neither shalt thou pollute thy Sabbath close !
" Mercy is safe and graceful.   How one hears
" The howl begin, scarce the three little taps   2060
" O' the silver mallet silent on thy brow,—
" ' His last act was to sacrifice a Count
" ' And thereby screen a scandal of the Church !
" ' Guido condemned, the Canon justified
" ' Of course,—delinquents of his cloth go free ! ' 2065
" And so the Luthers chuckle, Calvins scowl,
" So thy hand helps Molinos to the chair
" Whence he may hold forth till doom's day on just
" These *petit-maître* priestlings,—in the choir
" *Sanctus et Benedictus*, with a brush   2070
" Of soft guitar-strings that obey the thumb,
" Touched by the bedside, for accompaniment !
" Does this give umbrage to a husband?   Death
" To the fool, and to the priest impunity !
" But no impunity to any friend   2075

X.   L

" So simply over-loyal as these four
" Who made religion of their patron's cause,
" Believed in him and did his bidding straight,
" Asked not one question but laid down the lives
" This Pope took,—all four lives together make   2080
" Just his own length of days,—so, dead they lie,
" As these were times when loyalty 's a drug,
" And zeal in a subordinate too cheap
" And common to be saved when we spend life !
" Come, 't is too much good breath we waste in words :
" The pardon, Holy Father ! Spare grimace,   2086
" Shrugs and reluctance !   Are not we the world,
" Art not thou Priam? Let soft culture plead
" Hecuba-like, ' *non tali* ' (Virgil serves)
" '*Auxilio* ' and the rest !   Enough, it works !   2090
" The Pope relaxes, and the Prince is loth,
" The father's bowels yearn, the man's will bends,
" Reply is apt.   Our tears on tremble, hearts
" Big with a benediction, wait the word
" Shall circulate thro' the city in a trice,   2095
" Set every window flaring, give each man
" O' the mob his torch to wave for gratitude.
" Pronounce then, for our breath and patience fail ! "

I will, Sirs : but a voice other than yours
Quickens my spirit.   " *Quis pro Domino?*   2100

"Who is upon the Lord's side?" asked the Count.
I, who write—
           " On receipt of this command,
"Acquaint Count Guido and his fellows four
"They die to-morrow : could it be to-night,   2105
"The better, but the work to do, takes time.
"Set with all diligence a scaffold up,
"Not in the customary place, by Bridge
"Saint Angelo, where die the common sort;
"But since the man is noble, and his peers   2110
"By predilection haunt the People's Square,
"There let him be beheaded in the midst,
"And his companions hanged on either side :
"So shall the quality see, fear and learn.
"All which work takes time: till to-morrow, then,
"Let there be prayer incessant for the five!"   2116

For the main criminal I have no hope
Except in such a suddenness of fate.
I stood at Naples once, a night so dark
I could have scarce conjectured there was earth   2120
Anywhere, sky or sea or world at all :
But the night's black was burst through by a blaze—
Thunder struck blow on blow, earth groaned and bore,
Through her whole length of mountain visible :
There lay the city thick and plain with spires,   2125

L 2

And, like a ghost disshrouded, white the sea.
So may the truth be flashed out by one blow,
And Guido see, one instant, and be saved.
Else I avert my face, nor follow him
Into that sad obscure sequestered state   2130
Where God unmakes but to remake the soul
He else made first in vain ; which must not be.
Enough, for I may die this very night
And how should I dare die, this man let live?

Carry this forthwith to the Governor !   2135

XI.

GUIDO.

You are the Cardinal Acciaiuoli, and you,
Abate Panciatichi—two good Tuscan names:
Acciaiuoli—ah, your ancestor it was
Built the huge battlemented convent-block
Over the little forky flashing Greve   5
That takes the quick turn at the foot o' the hill
Just as one first sees Florence : oh those days !
'T is Ema, though, the other rivulet,
The one-arched brown brick bridge yawns over,—yes,
Gallop and go five minutes, and you gain   10
The Roman Gate from where the Ema 's bridged :
Kingfishers fly there : how I see the bend
O'erturreted by Certosa which he built,
That Senescal (we styled him) of your House !
I do adjure you, help me, Sirs !   My blood   15
Comes from as far a source : ought it to end
This way, by leakage through their scaffold-planks

Into Rome's sink where her red refuse runs?
Sirs, I beseech you by blood-sympathy,
If there be any vile experiment   20
In the air,—if this your visit simply prove,
When all 's done, just a well-intentioned trick
That tries for truth truer than truth itself,
By startling up a man, ere break of day,
To tell him he must die at sunset,—pshaw !   25
That man's a Franceschini ; feel his pulse,
Laugh at your folly, and let 's all go sleep !
You have my last word,—innocent am I
As Innocent my Pope and murderer,
Innocent as a babe, as Mary's own,   30
As Mary's self,—I said, say and repeat,—
And why, then, should I die twelve hours hence?   I—
Whom, not twelve hours ago, the gaoler bade
Turn to my straw-truss, settle and sleep sound
That I might wake the sooner, promptlier pay   35
His due of meat-and-drink-indulgence, cross
His palm with fee of the good-hand, beside,
As gallants use who go at large again !
For why?   All honest Rome approved my part ;
Whoever owned wife, sister, daughter,—nay,   40
Mistress,—had any shadow of any right
That looks like right, and, all the more resolved,
Held it with tooth and nail,—these manly men

Approved! I being for Rome, Rome was for me.
Then, there's the point reserved, the subterfuge   45
My lawyers held by, kept for last resource,
Firm should all else,—the impossible fancy!—fail,
And sneaking burgess-spirit win the day.
The knaves! One plea at least would hold,—they
          laughed,—
One grappling-iron scratch the bottom-rock   50
Even should the middle mud let anchor go!
I hooked my cause on to the Clergy's,—plea
Which, even if law tipped off my hat and plume,
Revealed my priestly tonsure, saved me so.
The Pope moreover, this old Innocent,   55
Being so meek and mild and merciful,
So fond o' the poor and so fatigued of earth,
So . . . fifty thousand devils in deepest hell!
Why must he cure us of our strange conceit
Of the angel in man's likeness, that we loved   60
And looked should help us at a pinch?   He help?
He pardon?   Here's his mind and message—death!
Thank the good Pope!   Now, is he good in this,
Never mind, Christian,—no such stuff's extant,—
But will my death do credit to his reign,   65
Show he both lived and let live, so was good?
Cannot I live if he but like?   "The law!"
Why, just the law gives him the very chance,

The precise leave to let my life alone,
Which the archangelic soul of him (he says)   70
Yearns after! Here they drop it in his palm,
My lawyers, capital o' the cursed kind,—
Drop life to take and hold and keep: but no!
He sighs, shakes head, refuses to shut hand,
Motions away the gift they bid him grasp,   75
And of the coyness comes—that off I run
And down I go, he best knows whither! mind,
He knows, who sets me rolling all the same!
Disinterested Vicar of our Lord,
This way he abrogates and disallows,   80
Nullifies and ignores,—reverts in fine
To the good and right, in detriment of me!
Talk away! Will you have the naked truth?
He 's sick of his life's supper,—swallowed lies:
So, hobbling bedward, needs must ease his maw   85
Just where I sit o' the door-sill. Sir Abate,
Can you do nothing? Friends, we used to frisk:
What of this sudden slash in a friend's face,
This cut across our good companionship
That showed its front so gay when both were young?
Were not we put into a beaten path,   91
Bid pace the world, we nobles born and bred,
We body of friends with each his scutcheon full
Of old achievement and impunity,—

Taking the laugh of morn and Sol's salute 95
As forth we fared, pricked on to breathe our steeds
And take equestrian sport over the green
Under the blue, across the crop,—what care?
If we went prancing up hill and down dale,
In and out of the level and the straight, 100
By the bit of pleasant byeway, where was harm?
Still Sol salutes me and the morning laughs:
I see my grandsire's hoof-prints,—point the spot
Where he drew rein, slipped saddle, and stabbed knave
For daring throw gibe—much less, stone—from pale: 105
Then back, and on, and up with the cavalcade.
Just so wend we, now canter, now converse,
Till, 'mid the jauncing pride and jaunty port,
Something of a sudden jerks at somebody—
A dagger is out, a flashing cut and thrust, 110
Because I play some prank my grandsire played,
And here I sprawl: where is the company? Gone!
A trot and a trample! only I lie trapped,
Writhe in a certain novel springe just set
By the good old Pope: I'm first prize. Warn me?
     Why? 115
Apprise me that the law o' the game is changed?
Enough that I'm a warning, as I writhe,
To all and each my fellows of the file,
And make law plain henceforward past mistake,

" For such a prank, death is the penalty ! "   120
Pope the Five Hundredth (what do I know or care?)
Deputes your Eminency and Abateship
To announce that, twelve hours from this time, he needs
I just essay upon my body and soul
The virtue of his brand-new engine, prove   125
Represser of the pranksome !   I 'm the first !
Thanks.   Do you know what teeth you mean to try
The sharpness of, on this soft neck and throat ?
I know it,—I have seen and hate it,—ay,
As you shall, while I tell you !   Let me talk,   130
Or leave me, at your pleasure ! talk I must :
What is your visit but my lure to talk?
Nay, you have something to disclose ?—a smile,
At end of the forced sternness, means to mock
The heart-beats here ?   I call your two hearts stone !
Is your charge to stay with me till I die?   136
Be tacit as your bench, then !   Use your ears,
I use my tongue : how glibly yours will run
At pleasant supper-time . . . God's curse ! . . . to-night
When all the guests jump up, begin so brisk   140
" Welcome, his Eminence who shrived the wretch !
" Now we shall have the Abate's story ! "

                                        Life !
How I could spill this overplus of mine

Among those hoar-haired, shrunk-shanked odds and
      ends
Of body and soul old age is chewing dry!   146
Those windlestraws that stare while purblind death
Mows here, mows there, makes hay of juicy me,
And misses just the bunch of withered weed
Would brighten hell and streak its smoke with flame!
How the life I could shed yet never shrink,   151
Would drench their stalks with sap like grass in May!
Is it not terrible, I entreat you, Sirs?—
With manifold and plenitudinous life,
Prompt at death's menace to give blow for threat, 155
Answer his " Be thou not! " by " Thus I am! "—
Terrible so to be alive yet die?

How I live, how I see! so,—how I speak!
Lucidity of soul unlocks the lips :
I never had the words at will before.   160
How I see all my folly at a glance!
" A man requires a woman and a wife : "
There was my folly; I believed the saw.
I knew that just myself concerned myself,
Yet needs must look for what I seemed to lack, 165
In a woman,—why, the woman 's in the man!
Fools we are, how we learn things when too late!
Overmuch life turns round my woman-side :

The male and female in me, mixed before,
Settle of a sudden: I 'm my wife outright   170
In this unmanly appetite for truth,
This careless courage as to consequence,
This instantaneous sight through things and through,
This voluble rhetoric, if you please,— 't is she!
Here you have that Pompilia whom I slew,   175
Also the folly for which I slew her!
                                        Fool!
And, fool-like, what is it I wander from?
What did I say of your sharp iron tooth?
Ah,—that I know the hateful thing! this way.   180
I chanced to stroll forth, many a good year gone,
One warm Spring eve in Rome, and unaware
Looking, mayhap, to count what stars were out,
Came on your fine axe in a frame, that falls
And so cuts off a man's head underneath,   185
Mannaia,—thus we made acquaintance first:
Out of the way, in a by-part o' the town,
At the Mouth-of-Truth o' the river-side, you know:
One goes by the Capitol: and wherefore coy,
Retiring out of crowded noisy Rome?   190
Because a very little time ago
It had done service, chopped off head from trunk
Belonging to a fellow whose poor house
The thing must make a point to stand before —

Felice Whatsoever-was-the-name   195
Who stabled buffaloes and so gained bread,
(Our clowns unyoke them in the ground hard by)
And, after use of much improper speech,
Had struck at Duke Some-title-or-other's face,
Because he kidnapped, carried away and kept   200
Felice's sister who would sit and sing
I' the filthy doorway while she plaited fringe
To deck the brutes with,—on their gear it goes,—
The good girl with the velvet in her voice.
So did the Duke, so did Felice, so   205
Did Justice, intervening with her axe.
There the man-mutilating engine stood
At ease, both gay and grim, like a Swiss guard
Off duty,—purified itself as well,
Getting dry, sweet and proper for next week,—   210
And doing incidental good, 't was hoped,
To the rough lesson-lacking populace
Who now and then, forsooth, must right their wrongs !
There stood the twelve-foot-square of scaffold, railed .
Considerately round to elbow-height,   215
For fear an officer should tumble thence
And sprain his ankle and be lame a month
Through starting when the axe fell and head too !
Railed likewise were the steps whereby 't was reached.
All of it painted red : red, in the midst,   220

Ran up two narrow tall beams barred across,
Since from the summit, some twelve feet to reach,
The iron plate with the sharp shearing edge
Had slammed, jerked, shot, slid,—I shall soon find
    which !—
And so lay quiet, fast in its fit place,   225
The wooden half-moon collar, now eclipsed
By the blade which blocked its curvature : apart,
The other half,—the under half-moon board
Which, helped by this, completes a neck's embrace,—
Joined to a sort of desk that wheels aside   230
Out of the way when done with,—down you kneel,
In you 're pushed, over you the other drops,
Tight you 're clipped, whiz, there 's the blade cleaves its
    best,
Out trundles body, down flops head on floor,
And where 's your soul gone ?   That, too, I shall find !
This kneeling-place was red, red, never fear !   236
But only slimy-like with paint, not blood,
For why? a decent pitcher stood at hand,
A broad dish to hold sawdust, and a broom
By some unnamed utensil,—scraper-rake,—   240
Each with a conscious air of duty done.
Underneath, loungers,—boys and some few men,—
Discoursed this platter, named the other tool,
Just as, when grooms tie up and dress a steed,

Boys lounge and look on, and elucubrate   245
What the round brush is used for, what the square,—
So was explained—to me the skill-less then—
The manner of the grooming for next world
Undergone by Felice What's-his-name.
There's no such lovely month in Rome as May—   250
May's crescent is no half-moon of red plank,
And came now tilting o'er the wave i' the west,
One greenish-golden sea, right 'twixt those bars
Of the engine—I began acquaintance with,
Understood, hated, hurried from before,   255
To have it out of sight and cleanse my soul !
Here it is all again, conserved for use :
Twelve hours hence, I may know more, not hate worse.

That young May-moon-month ! Devils of the deep !
Was not a Pope then Pope as much as now?   260
Used not he chirrup o'er the Merry Tales,
Chuckle,—his nephew so exact the wag
To play a jealous cullion such a trick
As wins the wife i' the pleasant story ! Well ?
Why do things change? Wherefore is Rome un-Romed?
I tell you, ere Felice's corpse was cold,   266
The Duke, that night, threw wide his palace-doors,
Received the compliments o' the quality
For justice done him,—bowed and smirked his best,

And in return passed round a pretty thing,   270
A portrait of Felice's sister's self,
Florid old rogue Albano's masterpiece,
As—better than virginity in rags—
Bouncing Europa on the back o' the bull :
They laughed and took their road the safelier home.
Ah, but times change, there 's quite another Pope,   276
I do the Duke's deed, take Felice's place,
And, being no Felice, lout and clout,
Stomach but ill the phrase " I lose my head ! "
How euphemistic ! Lose what ? Lose your ring,   280
Your snuff-box, tablets, kerchief !—but, your head ?
I learnt the process at an early age ;
'T was useful knowledge, in those same old days,
To know the way a head is set on neck.
My fencing-master urged " Would you excel ?   285
" Rest not content with mere bold give-and-guard,
" Nor pink the antagonist somehow-anyhow !
" See me dissect a little, and know your game !
" Only anatomy makes a thrust the thing."
Oh Cardinal, those lithe live necks of ours !   290
Here go the vertebræ, here 's *Atlas*, here
Axis, and here the symphyses stop short,
So wisely and well,—as, o'er a corpse, we cant,—
And here 's the silver cord which . . . what 's our word ?
Depends from the gold bowl, which loosed (not " lost ")

Lets us from heaven to hell,—one chop, we 're loose !
" And not much pain i' the process," quoth a sage :
Who told him? Not Felice's ghost, I think !
Such " losing " is scarce Mother Nature's mode.
She fain would have cord ease itself away,   300
Worn to a thread by threescore years and ten,
Snap while we slumber : that seems bearable.
I 'm told one clot of blood extravasate
Ends one as certainly as Roland's sword,—
One drop of lymph suffused proves Oliver's mace,— 305
Intruding, either of the pleasant pair,
On the arachnoid tunic of my brain.
That 's Nature's way of loosing cord !—but Art,
How of Art's process with the engine here,
When bowl and cord alike are crushed across,   310
Bored between, bruised through?   Why, if Fagon's
        self,
The French Court's pride, that famed practitioner,
Would pass his cold pale lightning of a knife,
Pistoja-ware, adroit 'twixt joint and joint,
With just a " See how facile, gentlefolk ! "—   315
The thing were not so bad to bear !   Brute force
Cuts as he comes, breaks in, breaks on, breaks out
O' the hard and soft of you : is that the same?
A lithe snake thrids the hedge, makes throb no leaf :
A heavy ox sets chest to brier and branch,   320

X.   M

Bursts somehow through, and leaves one hideous hole
Behind him !

And why, why must this needs be?
Oh, if men were but good !   They are not good,
Nowise like Peter : people called him rough,   · 325
But if, as I left Rome, I spoke the Saint,
—" *Petrus, quo vadis ?* "—doubtless, I should hear,
" To free the prisoner and forgive his fault !
" I plucked the absolute dead from God's own bar,
" And raised up Dorcas,—why not rescue thee? "   330
What would cost one such nullifying word ?
If Innocent succeeds to Peter's place,
Let him think Peter's thought, speak Peter's speech !
I say, he is bound to it : friends, how say you ?
Concede I be all one bloodguiltiness   335
And mystery of murder in the flesh,
Why should that fact keep the Pope's mouth shut fast?
He execrates my crime,—good !—sees hell yawn
One inch from the red plank's end which I press,—
Nothing is better !   What 's the consequence?   340
How should a Pope proceed that knows his cue ?
Why, leave me linger out my minute here,
Since close on death comes judgment and comes doom,
Not crib at dawn its pittance from a sheep
Destined ere dewfall to be butcher's-meat !   345

Think, Sirs, if I have done you any harm,
And you require the natural revenge,
Suppose, and so intend to poison me,
—Just as you take and slip into my draught
The paperful of powder that clears scores,   350
You notice on my brow a certain blue :
How you both overset the wine at once !
How you both smile ! " Our enemy has the plague !
" Twelve hours hence he 'll be scraping his bones bare
" Of that intolerable flesh, and die,   355
" Frenzied with pain : no need for poison here !
" Step aside and enjoy the spectacle ! "
Tender for souls are you, Pope Innocent !
Christ's maxim is—one soul outweighs the world :
Respite me, save a soul, then, curse the world !   360
" No," venerable sire, I hear you smirk,
" No : for Christ's gospel changes names, not things,
" Renews the obsolete, does nothing more !
" Our fire-new gospel is re-tinkered law,
" Our mercy, justice,—Jove 's rechristened God,—
" Nay, whereas, in the popular conceit,   366
" 'T is pity that old harsh Law somehow limps,
" Lingers on earth, although Law's day be done,
" Else would benignant Gospel interpose,
" Not furtively as now, but bold and frank   370
" O'erflutter us with healing in her wings,

M 2

" Law being harshness, Gospel only love —
" We tell the people, on the contrary,
" Gospel takes up the rod which Law lets fall ;
" Mercy is vigilant when justice sleeps !   375
ˠ Does Law permit a taste of Gospel-grace?
" The secular arm allow the spiritual power
" To act for once?—no compliment so fine
" As that our Gospel handsomely turn harsh,
" Thrust victim back on Law the nice and coy! "   380
Yes, you do say so, else you would forgive
Me whom Law does not touch but tosses you !
Don't think to put on the professional face !
You know what I know : casuists as you are,
Each nerve must creep, each hair start, sting and stand,
At such illogical inconsequence !   386
Dear my friends, do but see !   A murder 's tried,
There are two parties to the cause : I 'm one,
—Defend myself, as somebody must do :
I have the best o' the battle : that 's a fact,   390
Simple fact,—fancies find no place just now.
What though half Rome condemned me? Half approved :
And, none disputes, the luck is mine at last,
All Rome, i' the main, acquitting me : whereon,
What has the Pope to ask but " How finds Law? "   395
" I find," replies Law, " I have erred this while :
" Guilty or guiltless, Guido proves a priest,

" No layman : he is therefore yours, not mine :
" I bound him : loose him, you whose will is Christ's ! "
And now what does this Vicar of our Lord,   400
Shepherd o' the flock,—one of whose charge bleats sore
For crook's help from the quag wherein it drowns?
Law suffers him employ the crumpled end :
His pleasure is to turn staff, use the point,
And thrust the shuddering sheep, he calls a wolf,   405
Back and back, down and down to where hell gapes !
" Guiltless," cries Law—" Guilty " corrects the Pope !
" Guilty," for the whim's sake !   " Guilty," he somehow
     thinks,
And anyhow says : 't is truth ; he dares not lie !

Others should do the lying.   That 's the cause   410
Brings you both here : I ought in decency
Confess to you that I deserve my fate,
Am guilty, as the Pope thinks,—ay, to the end,
Keep up the jest, lie on, lie ever, lie
I' the latest gasp of me !   What reason, Sirs?   415
Because to-morrow will succeed to-day
For you, though not for me : and if I stick
Still to the truth, declare with my last breath,
I die an innocent and murdered man,—
Why, there 's the tongue of Rome will wag apace   420
This time to-morrow : don't I hear the talk !

" So, to the last he proved impenitent?

" Pagans have said as much of martyred saints !

" Law demurred, washed her hands of the whole case.

" Prince Somebody said this, Duke Something, that. 425

" Doubtless the man 's dead, dead enough, don't fear !

" But, hang it, what if there have been a spice,

' A touch of . . . eh?   You see, the Pope 's so old,

" Some of us add, obtuse : age never slips

" The chance of shoving youth to face death first ! "   430

And so on.   Therefore to suppress such talk

You two come here, entreat I tell you lies,

And end, the edifying way.   I end,

Telling the truth !   Your self-styled shepherd thieves !

A thief—and how thieves hate the wolves we know : 435

Damage to theft, damage to thrift, all 's one !

The red hand is sworn foe of the black jaw.

That 's only natural, that 's right enough :

But why the wolf should compliment the thief

With shepherd's title, bark out life in thanks,   440

And, spiteless, lick the prong that spits him,—eh,

Cardinal?   My Abate, scarcely thus !

There, let my sheepskin-garb, a curse on 't, go—

Leave my teeth free if I must show my shag !

Repent?   What good shall follow?   If I pass   445

Twelve hours repenting, will that fact hold fast

The thirteenth at the horrid dozen's end?

If I fall forthwith at your feet, gnash, tear,
Foam, rave, to give your story the due grace,
Will that assist the engine half-way back   450
Into its hiding-house?—boards, shaking now,
Bone against bone, like some old skeleton bat
That wants, at winter's end, to wake and prey!
Will howling put the spectre back to sleep?
Ah, but I misconceive your object, Sirs!   455
Since I want new life like the creature,—life,
Being done with here, begins i' the world away:
I shall next have " Come, mortals, and be judged!"
There 's but a minute betwixt this and then:
So, quick, be sorry since it saves my soul!   460
Sirs, truth shall save it, since no lies assist!
Hear the truth, you, whatever you style yourselves,
Civilization and society!
Come, one good grapple, I with all the world!
Dying in cold blood is the desperate thing;   465
The angry heart explodes, bears off in blaze
The indignant soul, and I 'm combustion-ripe.
Why, you intend to do your worst with me!
That 's in your eyes! You dare no more than death,
And mean no less. I must make up my mind.   470
So Pietro,—when I chased him here and there,
Morsel by morsel cut away the life
I loathed,—cried for just respite to confess

And save his soul: much respite did I grant!
Why grant me respite who deserve my doom?   475
Me—who engaged to play a prize, fight you,
Knowing your arms, and foil you, trick for trick,
At rapier-fence, your match and, maybe, more.
I knew that if I chose sin certain sins,
Solace my lusts out of the regular way   480
Prescribed me, I should find you in the path,
Have to try skill with a redoubted foe;
You would lunge, I would parry, and make end.
At last, occasion of a murder comes:
We cross blades, I, for all my brag, break guard, 485
And in goes the cold iron at my breast,
Out at my back, and end is made of me.
You stand confessed the adroiter swordsman,—ay,
But on your triumph you increase, it seems,
Want more of me than lying flat on face: 490
I ought to raise my ruined head, allege
Not simply I pushed worse blade o' the pair,
But my antagonist dispensed with steel!
There was no passage of arms, you looked me low,
With brow and eye abolished cut and thrust   495
Nor used the vulgar weapon!   This chance scratch,
This incidental hurt, this sort of hole
I' the heart of me?   I stumbled, got it so!
Fell on my own sword as a bungler may!

Yourself proscribe such heathen tools, and trust 500
To the naked virtue : it was virtue stood
Unarmed and awed me,—on my brow there burned
Crime out so plainly intolerably red,
That I was fain to cry—" Down to the dust
" With me, and bury there brow, brand and all ! " 505
Law had essayed the adventure,—but what 's Law?
Morality exposed the Gorgon shield !
Morality and Religion conquer me.
If Law sufficed would you come here, entreat
I supplement law, and confess forsooth? 510
Did not the Trial show things plain enough?
" Ah, but a word of the man's very self
" Would somehow put the keystone in its place
" And crown the arch ! " Then take the word you want !

I say that, long ago, when things began, 515
All the world made agreement, such and such
Were pleasure-giving profit-bearing acts,
But henceforth extra-legal, nor to be :
You must not kill the man whose death would please
And profit you, unless his life stop yours 520
Plainly, and need so be put aside :
Get the thing by a public course, by law,
Only no private bloodshed as of old !
All of us, for the good of every one,

Renounced such licence and conformed to law :   525
Who breaks law, breaks pact therefore, helps himself
To pleasure and profit over and above the due,
And must pay forfeit,—pain beyond his share :
For, pleasure being the sole good in the world,
Anyone's pleasure turns to someone's pain,   530
So, law must watch for everyone,—say we,
Who call things wicked that give too much joy,
And nickname mere reprisal, envy makes,
Punishment : quite right ! thus the world goes round.
I, being well aware such pact there was,   535
I, in my time who found advantage come
Of law's observance and crime's penalty,—
Who, but for wholesome fear law bred in friends,
Had doubtless given example long ago,
Furnished forth some friend's pleasure with my pain,
And, by my death, pieced out his scanty life,—   541
I could not, for that foolish life of me,
Help risking law's infringement,—I broke bond,
And needs must pay price,—wherefore, here's my head,
Flung with a flourish !   But, repentance too?   545
But pure and simple sorrow for law's breach
Rather than blunderer's-ineptitude?
Cardinal, no !   Abate, scarcely thus !
'T is the fault, not that I dared try a fall
With Law and straightway am found undermost,   550

But that I failed to see, above man's law,
God's precept you, the Christians, recognize?
Colly my cow!   Don't fidget, Cardinal!
Abate, cross your breast and count your beads
And exorcize the devil, for here he stands   555
And stiffens in the bristly nape of neck,
Daring you drive him hence!   You, Christians both?
I say, if ever was such faith at all
Born in the world, by your community
Suffered to live its little tick of time,   560
'T is dead of age, now, ludicrously dead;
Honour its ashes, if you be discreet,
In epitaph only!   For, concede its death,
Allow extinction, you may boast unchecked
What feats the thing did in a crazy land   565
At a fabulous epoch,—treat your faith, that way,
Just as you treat your relics: " Here 's a shred
" Of saintly flesh, a scrap of blessed bone,
" Raised King Cophetua, who was dead, to life
" In Mesopotamy twelve centuries since,   570
" Such was its virtue!"—twangs the Sacristan,
Holding the shrine-box up, with hands like feet
Because of gout in every finger joint:
Does he bethink him to reduce one knob,
Allay one twinge by touching what he vaunts?   575
I think he half uncrooks fist to catch fee,

But, for the grace, the quality of cure,—
Cophetua was the man put that to proof !
Not otherwise, your faith is shrined and shown
And shamed at once : you banter while you bow ! 580
Do you dispute this?   Come, a monster-laugh,
A madman's laugh, allowed his Carnival
Later ten days than when all Rome, but he,
Laughed at the candle-contest : mine's alight,
'T is just it sputter till the puff o' the Pope   585
End it to-morrow and the world turn Ash.
Come, thus I wave a wand and bring to pass
In a moment, in the twinkle of an eye,
What but that—feigning everywhere grows fact,
Professors turn possessors, realize   590
The faith they play with as a fancy now,
And bid it operate, have full effect
On every circumstance of life, to-day,
In Rome,—faith's flow set free at fountain-head !
Now, you 'll own, at this present, when I speak,   595
Before I work the wonder, there 's no man
Woman or child in Rome, faith's fountain-head,
But might, if each were minded, realize
Conversely unbelief, faith's opposite—
Set it to work on life unflinchingly,   600
Yet give no symptom of an outward change :
Why should things change because men disbelieve

What 's incompatible, in the whited tomb,
With bones and rottenness one inch below?
What saintly act is done in Rome to-day   605
But might be prompted by the devil,—" is "
I say not,—" has been, and again may be,—"
I do say, full i' the face o' the crucifix
You try to stop my mouth with! Off with it!
Look in your own heart, if your soul have eyes! 610
You shall see reason why, though faith were fled,
Unbelief still might work the wires and move
Man, the machine, to play a faithful part.
Preside your college, Cardinal, in your cape,
Or,—having got above his head, grown Pope,— 615
Abate, gird your loins and wash my feet!
Do you suppose I am at loss at all
Why you crook, why you cringe, why fast or feast?
Praise, blame, sit, stand, lie or go!—all of it,
In each of you, purest unbelief may prompt,   620
And wit explain to who has eyes to see.
But, lo, I wave wand, made the false the true!
Here 's Rome believes in Christianity!
What an explosion, how the fragments fly
Of what was surface, mask and make-believe!   625
Begin now,—look at this Pope's-halberdier
In wasp-like black and yellow foolery!
He, doing duty at the corridor,

Wakes from a muse and stands convinced of sin !
Down he flings halbert, leaps the passage-length,   630
Pushes into the presence, pantingly
Submits the extreme peril of the case
To the Pope's self,—whom in the world beside?—
And the Pope breaks talk with ambassador,
Bids aside bishop, wills the whole world wait   635
Till he secure that prize, outweighs the world,
A soul, relieve the sentry of his qualm !
His Altitude the Referendary,—
Robed right, and ready for the usher's word
To pay devoir,—is, of all times, just then   640
'Ware of a master-stroke of argument
Will cut the spinal cord . . , ugh, ugh ! . . . I mean,
Paralyse Molinism for evermore !
Straight he leaves lobby, trundles, two and two,
Down steps to reach home, write, if but a word   645
Shall end the impudence : he leaves who likes
Go pacify the Pope : there 's Christ to serve !
How otherwise would men display their zeal?
If the same sentry had the least surmise
A powder-barrel 'neath the pavement lay   650
In neighbourhood with what might prove a match,
Meant to blow sky-high Pope and presence both—
Would he not break through courtiers, rank and file,
Bundle up, bear off and save body so,

The Pope, no matter for his priceless soul? 655
There 's no fool's-freak here, nought to soundly swinge,
Only a man in earnest, you 'll so praise
And pay and prate about, that earth shall ring!
Had thought possessed the Referendary
His jewel-case at home was left ajar, 660
What would be wrong in running, robes awry,
To be beforehand with the pilferer?
What talk then of indecent haste? Which means,
That both these, each in his degree, would do
Just that,—for a comparative nothing's sake, 665
And thereby gain approval and reward,—
Which, done for what Christ says is worth the world, '
Procures the doer curses, cuffs and kicks.
I call such difference 'twixt act and act,
Sheer lunacy unless your truth on lip 670
Be recognized a lie in heart of you!
How do you all act, promptly or in doubt,
When there 's a guest poisoned at supper-time
And he sits chatting on with spot on cheek?
"Pluck him by the skirt, and round him in the ears,
"Have at him by the beard, warn anyhow!" 676
Good, and this other friend that 's cheat and thief
And dissolute,—go stop the devil's feast,
Withdraw him from the imminent hell-fire!
Why, for your life, you dare not tell your friend 680

"You lie, and I admonish you for Christ!"
Who yet dare seek that same man at the Mass
To warn him—on his knees, and tinkle near,—
He left a cask a-tilt, a tap unturned,
The Trebbian running: what a grateful jump   685
Out of the Church rewards your vigilance!
Perform that self-same service just a thought
More maladroitly,—since a bishop sits
At function!—and he budges not, bites lip,—
"You see my case: how can I quit my post?   690
"He has an eye to any such default.
"See to it, neighbour, I beseech your love!"
He and you know the relative worth of things,
What is permissible or inopportune.   694
Contort your brows! You know I speak the truth:
Gold is called gold, and dross called dross, i' the Book:
Gold you let lie and dross pick up and prize!
—Despite your muster of some fifty monks
And nuns a-maundering here and mumping there,
Who could, and on occasion would, spurn dross,   700
Clutch gold, and prove their faith a fact so far,—
I grant you! Fifty times the number squeak
And gibber in the madhouse—firm of faith,
This fellow, that his nose supports the moon;
The other, that his straw hat crowns him Pope: 705
Does that prove all the world outside insane?

Do fifty miracle-mongers match the mob
That acts on the frank faithless principle,
Born-baptized-and-bred Christian-atheists, each
With just as much a right to judge as you,—   710
As many senses in his soul, and nerves
I' neck of him as I,—whom, soul and sense,
Neck and nerve, you abolish presently,—
I being the unit in creation now
Who pay the Maker, in this speech of mine,   715
A creature's duty, spend my last of breath
In bearing witness, even by my worst fault,
To the creature's obligation, absolute,
Perpetual: my worst fault protests, " The faith
" Claims all of me : I would give all she claims,
" But for a spice of doubt : the risk 's too rash : 721
" Double or quits, I play, but, all or nought,
" Exceeds my courage : therefore, I descend
" To the next faith with no dubiety—
" Faith in the present life, made last as long   725
" And prove as full of pleasure as may hap,
" Whatever pain it cause the world."   I 'm wrong?
I 've had my life, whate'er I lose : I 'm right ?
I 've got the single good there was to gain.
Entire faith, or else complete unbelief !   730
Aught between has my loathing and contempt,
Mine and God's also, doubtless : ask yourself,

X.   N

Cardinal, where and how you like a man!
Why, either with your feet upon his head,
Confessed your caudatory, or, at large,   735
The stranger in the crowd who caps to you
But keeps his distance,—why should he presume?
You want no hanger-on and dropper-off,
Now yours, and now not yours but quite his own,
According as the sky looks black or bright.   740
Just so I capped to and kept off from faith—
You promised trudge behind through fair and foul,
Yet leave i' the lurch at the first spit of rain.
Who holds to faith whenever rain begins?
What does the father when his son lies dead,   745
The merchant when his money-bags take wing,
The politician whom a rival ousts?
No case but has its conduct, faith prescribes:
Where 's the obedience that shall edify?
Why, they laugh frankly in the face of faith   750
And take the natural course,—this rends his hair
Because his child is taken to God's breast,
That gnashes teeth and raves at loss of trash
Which rust corrupts and thieves break through and steal,
And this, enabled to inherit earth   755
Through meekness, curses till your blood runs cold!
Down they all drop to my low level, rest
Heart upon dungy earth that 's warm and soft,

And let who please attempt the altitudes.
Each playing prodigal son of heavenly sire,   760
Turning his nose up at the fatted calf,
Fain to fill belly with the husks, we swine
Did eat by born depravity of taste!

Enough of the hypocrites. But you, Sirs, you—
Who never budged from litter where I lay,   765
And buried snout i' the draff-box while I fed,
Cried amen to my creed's one article—
" Get pleasure, 'scape pain,—give your preference
" To the immediate good, for time is brief,
" And death ends good and ill and everything!   770
" What 's got is gained, what 's gained soon is gained twice,
" And,—inasmuch as faith gains most,—feign faith ! "
So did we brother-like pass word about :
—You, now,—like bloody drunkards but half-drunk,
Who fool men yet perceive men find them fools,— 775
Vexed that a titter gains the gravest mouth,—
O' the sudden you must needs re-introduce
Solemnity, straight sober undue mirth
By a blow dealt me your boon companion here
Who, using the old licence, dreamed of harm   780
No more than snow in harvest : yet it falls !
You check the merriment effectually
By pushing your abrupt machine i' the midst,

Making me Rome's example : blood for wine !
The general good needs that you chop and change ! 785
I may dislike the hocus-pocus,—Rome,
The laughter-loving people, won't they stare
Chap-fallen !—while serious natures sermonize
" The magistrate, he beareth not the sword
" In vain ; who sins may taste its edge, we see ! "   790
Why my sin, drunkards ?   Where have I abused
Liberty, scandalized you all so much?
Who called me, who crooked finger till I came,
Fool that I was, to join companionship ?
I knew my own mind, meant to live my life,   795
Elude your envy, or else make a stand,
Take my own part and sell you my life dear.
But it was " Fie !   No prejudice in the world
" To the proper manly instinct !   Cast your lot
" Into our lap, one genius ruled our births,   800
" We 'll compass joy by concert ; take with us
" The regular irregular way i' the wood ;
" You 'll miss no game through riding breast by breast,
" In this preserve, the Church's park and pale,
" Rather than outside where the world lies waste ! "   805
Come, if you said not that, did you say this ?
Give plain and terrible warning, " Live, enjoy ?
" Such life begins in death and ends in hell !
" Dare you bid us assist your sins, us priests

"Who hurry sin and sinners from the earth? 810
"No such delight for us, why then for you?
"Leave earth, seek heaven or find its opposite!"
Had you so warned me, not in lying words
But veritable deeds with tongues of flame,
That had been fair, that might have struck a man,
Silenced the squabble between soul and sense, 816
Compelled him to make mind up, take one course
Or the other, peradventure!—wrong or right,
Foolish or wise, you would have been at least
Sincere, no question,—forced me choose, indulge 820
Or else renounce my instincts, still play wolf
Or find my way submissive to your fold,
Be red-crossed on my fleece, one sheep the more.
But you as good as bade me wear sheep's wool
Over wolf's skin, suck blood and hide the noise 825
By mimicry of something like a bleat,—
Whence it comes that because, despite my care,
Because I smack my tongue too loud for once,
Drop baaing, here 's the village up in arms!
Have at the wolf's throat, you who hate the breed!
Oh, were it only open yet to choose— 831
One little time more—whether I 'd be free
Your foe, or subsidized your friend forsooth!
Should not you get a growl through the white fangs
In answer to your beckoning! Cardinal, 835

Abate, managers o' the multitude,
I 'd turn your gloved hands to account, be sure!
You should manipulate the coarse rough mob:
'T is you I 'd deal directly with, not them,—
Using your fears: why touch the thing myself   840
When I could see you hunt, and then cry "Shares!
" Quarter the carcase or we quarrel; come,
" Here 's the world ready to see justice done!"
Oh, it had been a desperate game, but game
Wherein the winner's chance were worth the pains!
We 'd try conclusions!—at the worst, what worse ·846
Than this Mannaia-machine, each minute's talk
Helps push an inch the nearer me? Fool, fool!

You understand me and forgive, sweet Sirs?
I blame you, tear my hair and tell my woe—   850
All 's but a flourish, figure of rhetoric!
One must try each expedient to save life.
One makes fools look foolisher fifty-fold
By putting in their place men wise like you,
To take the full force of an argument   855
Would buffet their stolidity in vain.
If you should feel aggrieved by the mere wind
O' the blow that means to miss you and maul them,
That 's my success! Is it not folly, now,
To say with folk, " A plausible defence—   860

" We see through notwithstanding, and reject ? "
Reject the plausible they do, these fools,
Who never even make pretence to show
One point beyond its plausibility
In favour of the best belief they hold !   865
" Saint Somebody-or-other raised the dead : "
Did he ?   How do you come to know as much ?
" Know it, what need ?   The story's plausible,
" Avouched for by a martyrologist,
" And why should good men sup on cheese and leeks
" On such a saint's day, if there were no saint ? " 871
I praise the wisdom of these fools, and straight
Tell them my story—" plausible, but false ! "
False, to be sure ! What else can story be
That runs—a young wife tired of an old spouse, 875
Found a priest whom she fled away with,—both
Took their full pleasure in the two-days' flight,
Which a grey-headed greyer-hearted pair,
(Whose best boast was, their life had been a lie)
Helped for the love they bore all liars. Oh, 880
Here incredulity begins ! Indeed ?
Allow then, were no one point strictly true,
There 's that i' the tale might seem like truth at least
To the unlucky husband,—jaundiced patch —
Jealousy maddens people, why not him ? 885
Say, he was maddened, so forgivable !

Humanity pleáds that though the wife were true,
The priest true, and the pair of liars true,
They might seem false to one man in the world!
A thousand gnats make up a serpent's sting,   890
And many sly soft stimulants to wrath
Compose a formidable wrong at last
That gets called easily by some one name
Not applicable to the single parts,
And so draws down a general revenge,   895
Excessive if you take crime, fault by fault.
Jealousı! I have known a score of plays,
Were listened to and laughed at in my time
As like the everyday-life on all sides,
Wherein the husband, mad as a March hare,   900
Suspected all the world contrived his shame.
What did the wife?   The wife kissed both eyes blind,
Explained away ambiguous circumstance,
And while she held him captive by the hand,
Crowned his head,—you know what's the mockery,—
By half her body behind the curtain.   That's   906
Nature now!   That's the subject of a piece
I saw in Vallombrosa Convent, made
Expressly to teach men what marriage was!
But say " Just so did I misapprehend,   910
" Imagine she deceived me to my face,"
And that's pretence too easily seen through!

All those eyes of all husbands in all plays,
At stare like one expanded peacock-tail,
Are laughed at for pretending to be keen   915
While horn-blind: but the moment I step forth—
Oh, I must needs o' the sudden prove a lynx
And look the heart, that stone-wall, through and
          through!
Such an eye, God's may be,—not yours nor mine.

Yes, presently .   . what hour is fleeting now? 920
When you cut earth away from under me,
I shall be left alone with, pushed beneath
Some such an apparitional dread orb
As the eye of God, since such an eye there glares:
I fancy it go filling up the void   925
Above my mote-self it devours, or what
Proves—wrath, immensity wreaks on nothingness.
Just how I felt once, couching through the dark,
Hard by Vittiano; young I was, and gay,
And wanting to trap fieldfares: first a spark   930
Tipped a bent, as a mere dew-globule might
Any stiff grass-stalk on the meadow,—this
Grew fiercer, flamed out full, and proved the sun.
What do I want with proverbs, precepts here?
Away with man!   What shall I say to God?   935
This, if I find the tongue and keep the mind—

"Do Thou wipe out the being of me, and smear
"This soul from off Thy white of things, I blot!
"I am one huge and sheer mistake,—whose fault?
"Not mine at least, who did not make myself!" 940
Someone declares my wife excused me so!
Perhaps she knew what argument to use.
Grind your teeth, Cardinal: Abate, writhe!
What else am I to cry out in my rage,
Unable to repent one particle   945
O' the past? Oh, how I wish some cold wise man
Would dig beneath the surface which you scrape,
Deal with the depths, pronounce on my desert
Groundedly! I want simple sober sense,
That asks, before it finishes with a dog,   950
Who taught the dog that trick you hang him for?
You both persist to call that act a crime,
Which sense would call . . . yes, I maintain it, Sirs, . . .
A blunder! At the worst, I stood in doubt
On cross-road, took one path of many paths: 955
It leads to the red thing, we all see now,
But nobody saw at first: one primrose-patch
In bank, one singing-bird in bush, the less,
Had warned me from such wayfare: let me prove!
Put me back to the cross-road, start afresh! 960
Advise me when I take the first false step!
Give me my wife: how should I use my wife,

Love her or hate her? Prompt my action now!
There she is, there she stands alive and pale,
The thirteen-years'·old child, with milk for blood,
Pompilia Comparini, as at first,   966
Which first is only four brief years ago!
I stand too in the little ground-floor room
O' the father's house at Via Vittoria: see!
Her so-called mother,—one arm round the waist 970
O' the child to keep her from the toys, let fall
At wonder I can live yet look so grim,—
Ushers her in, with deprecating wave
Of the other,—and she fronts me loose at last,
Held only by the mother's finger-tip.   975
Struck dumb,—for she was white enough before!—
· She eyes me with those frightened balls of black,
As heifer—the old simile comes pat—
Eyes tremblingly the altar and the priest.
The amazed look, all one insuppressive prayer,— 980
Might she but breathe, set free as heretofore,
Have this cup leave her lips unblistered, bear
Any cross anywhither anyhow,
So but alone, so but apart from me!
You are touched? So am I, quite otherwise,   985
If 't is with pity. I resent my wrong,
Being a man: I only show man's soul
Through man's flesh: she sees mine, it strikes her thus!

Is that attractive? To a youth perhaps—
Calf-creature, one-part boy to three-parts girl,   990
To whom it is a flattering novelty
That he, men use to motion from their path,
Can thus impose, thus terrify in turn
A chit whose terror shall be changed apace
To bliss unbearable when grace and glow,   995
Prowess and pride descend the throne and touch
Esther in all that pretty tremble, cured
By the dove o' the sceptre !   But myself am old,
O' the wane at least, in all things : what do you say
To her who frankly thus confirms my doubt?   1000
I am past the prime, I scare the woman-world,
Done-with that way : you like this piece of news?
A little saucy rose-bud minx can strike
Death-damp into the breast of doughty king   1004
Though 't were French Louis,—soul I understand,—
Saying, by gesture of repugnance, just
" Sire, you are regal, puissant and so forth,
" But—young you have been, are not, nor will be ! "
In vain the mother nods, winks, bustles up,
" Count, girls incline to mature worth like you !   1010
" As for Pompilia, what 's flesh, fish, or fowl
" To one who apprehends no difference,
" And would accept you even were you old
" As you are . . . youngish by her father's side ?

"Trim but your beard a little, thin your bush   1015
" Of eyebrow; and for presence, portliness,
" And decent gravity, you beat a boy ! "
Deceive yourself one minute, if you may,
In presence of the child that so loves age,   1019
Whose neck writhes, cords itself against your kiss,
Whose hand you wring stark, rigid with despair !
Well, I resent this; I am young in soul,
Nor old in body,—thews and sinews here,—
Though the vile surface be not smooth as once,—
Far beyond that first wheelwork which went wrong
Through the untempered iron ere 't was proof :   1026
I am the wrought man worth ten times the crude,
Would woman see what this declines to see,
Declines to say " I see,"—the officious word
That makes the thing, pricks on the soul to shoot
New fire into the half-used cinder, flesh !   1031
Therefore 't is she begins with wronging me,
Who cannot but begin with hating her.
Our marriage follows : there she stands again !
Why do I laugh?   Why, in the very gripe   1035
O' the jaws of death's gigantic skull, do I
Grin back his grin, make sport of my own pangs?
Why from each clashing of his molars, ground
To make the devil bread from out my grist,
Leaps out a spark of mirth, a hellish toy ?   1040

Take notice we are lovers in a church,
Waiting the sacrament to make us one
And happy !   Just as bid, she bears herself,
Comes and kneels, rises, speaks, is silent,—goes :
So have I brought my horse, by word and blow,   1045
To stand stock-still and front the fire he dreads.
How can I other than remember this,
Resent the very obedience ?   Gain thereby ?
Yes, I do gain my end and have my will,—
Thanks to whom ?   When the mother speaks the word,
She obeys it—even to enduring me !   1051
There had been compensation in revolt—
Revolt 's to quell : but martyrdom rehearsed,
But predetermined saintship for the sake
O' the mother ?—" Go ! " thought I, " we meet again ! "
Pass the next weeks of dumb contented death,   1056
She lives,—wakes up, installed in house and home,
Is mine, mine all day-long, all night-long mine.
Good folk begin at me with open mouth
" Now, at least, reconcile the child to life !   1060
" Study and make her love . . . that is, endure
" The . . . hem ! the . . . all of you though somewhat
       old,
" Till it amount to something, in her eye,
" As good as love, better a thousand times,—
" Since nature helps the woman in such strait,   1065

" Makes passiveness her pleasure : failing which,
" What if you give up boy-and-girl-fools'-play
" And go on to wise friendship all at once ?
" Those boys and girls kiss themselves cold, you know,
" Toy themselves tired and slink aside full soon   1070
" To friendship, as they name satiety :
" Thither go you and wait their coming ! "   Thanks,
Considerate advisers,—but, fair play !
Had you and I, friends, started fair at first
We, keeping fair, might reach it, neck by neck,   1075
This blessed goal, whenever fate so please :
But why am I to miss the daisied mile
The course begins with, why obtain the dust
Of the end precisely at the starting-point?
Why quaff life's cup blown free of all the beads,   1080
The bright red froth wherein our beard should steep
Before our mouth essay the black o' the wine?
Foolish, the love-fit?   Let me prove it such
Like you, before like you I puff things clear !
" The best 's to come, no rapture but content !   1085
" Not love's first glory but a sober glow,
" Not a spontaneous outburst in pure boon,
" So much as, gained by patience, care and toil,
" Proper appreciation and esteem ! "
Go preach that to your nephews, not to me   1090
Who, tired i' the midway of my life, would stop

And take my first refreshment, pluck a rose :
What 's this coarse woolly hip, worn smooth of leaf,
You counsel I go plant in garden-plot,
Water with tears, manure with sweat and blood,   1095
In confidence the seed shall germinate
And, for its very best, some far-off day,
Grow big, and blow me out a dog-rose bell ?
Why must your nephews begin breathing spice
O' the hundred-petalled Provence prodigy?   1100
Nay, more and worse,—would such my root bear rose—
Prove really flower and favourite, not the kind
That 's queen, but those three leaves that make one cup
And hold the hedge-bird's breakfast,—then indeed
The prize though poor would pay the care and toil !   1105
Respect we Nature that makes least as most,
Marvellous in the minim !   But this bud,
Bit through and burned black by the tempter's tooth,
This bloom whose best grace was the slug outside
And the wasp inside its bosom,—call you "rose " ?   1110
Claim no immunity from a weed's fate
For the horrible present !   What you call my wife
I call a nullity in female shape,
Vapid disgust, soon to be pungent plague,
When mixed with, made confusion and a curse   1115
By two abominable nondescripts,
That father and that mother : think you see

The dreadful bronze our boast, we Aretines,
The Etruscan monster, the three-headed thing,
Bellerophon's foe ! How name you the whole beast ?
You choose to name the body from one head,   1121
That of the simple kid which droops the eye,
Hangs the neck and dies tenderly enough:
I rather see the griesly lion belch
Flame out i' the midst, the serpent writhe her rings,
Grafted into the common stock for tail,   1126
And name the brute, Chimæra which I slew !
How was there ever more to be—(concede
My wife's insipid harmless nullity)—
Dissociation from that pair of plagues—   1130
That mother with her cunning and her cant—
The eyes with first their twinkle of conceit,
Then, dropped to earth in mock-demureness,—now,
The smile self-satisfied from ear to ear,
Now, the prim pursed-up mouth's protruded lips, 1135
With deferential duck, slow swing of head,
Tempting the sudden fist of man too much,—
That owl-like screw of lid and rock of ruff !
As for the father,—Cardinal, you know,
The kind of idiot !—such are rife in Rome,   1140
But they wear velvet commonly ; good fools,
At the end of life, to furnish forth young folk
Who grin and bear with imbecility :

x.   o

Since the stalled ass, the joker, sheds from jaw
Corn, in the joke, for those who laugh or starve. 1145
But what say we to the same solemn beast
Wagging his ears and wishful of our pat,
When turned, with holes in hide and bones laid bare,
To forage for himself i' the waste o' the world,
Sir Dignity i' the dumps?   Pat him?   We drub 1150
Self-knowledge, rather, into frowzy pate,
Teach Pietro to get trappings or go hang!
Fancy this quondam oracle in vogue
At Via Vittoria, this personified
Authority when time was,—Pantaloon   1155
Flaunting his tom-fool tawdry just the same
As if Ash-Wednesday were mid-Carnival!
That 's the extreme and unforgiveable
Of sins, as I account such.   Have you stooped
For your own ends to bestialize yourself   1160
By flattery of a fellow of this stamp?
The ends obtained or else shown out of reach,
He goes on, takes the flattery for pure truth,—
" You love, and honour me, of course: what next?"
What, but the trifle of the stabbing, friend?—   1165
Which taught you how one worships when the shrine
Has lost the relic that we bent before.
Angry!   And how could I be otherwise?
'T is plain: this pair of old pretentious fools

Meant to fool me : it happens, I fooled them.   1170
Why could not these who sought to buy and sell
Me,—when they found themselves were bought and sold,
Make up their mind to the proved rule of right,
Be chattel and not chapman any more ?
Miscalculation has its consequence ;   1175
But when the shepherd crooks a sheep-like thing
And meaning to get wool, dislodges fleece
And finds the veritable wolf beneath,
(How that staunch image serves at every turn !)
Does he, by way of being politic,   1180
Pluck the first whisker grimly visible ?
Or rather grow in a trice all gratitude,
Protest this sort-of-what-one-might-name sheep
Beats the old other curly-coated kind,
And shall share board and bed, if so it deign,   1185
With its discoverer, like a royal ram ?
Ay, thus, with chattering teeth and knocking knees,
Would wisdom treat the adventure ! these, forsooth,
Tried whisker-plucking, and so found what trap
The whisker kept perdue, two rows of teeth—   1190
Sharp, as too late the prying fingers felt.
What would you have ?   The fools transgress, the fools
Forthwith receive appropriate punishment :
They first insult me, I return the blow,
There follows noise enough : four hubbub months, 1195

Now hue and cry, now whimpering and wail—
A perfect goose-yard cackle of complaint
Because I do not gild the geese their oats,—
I have enough of noise, ope wicket wide,
Sweep out the couple to go whine elsewhere,   1200
Frightened a little, hurt in no respect,
And am just taking thought to breathe again,
Taste the sweet sudden silence all about,
When, there they raise it, the old noise I know,
At Rome i' the distance !   " What, begun once more ?
" Whine on, wail ever, 't is the loser's right ! "   1206
But eh, what sort of voice grows on the wind?
Triumph it sounds and no complaint at all !
And triumph it is.   My boast was premature :
The creatures, I turned forth, clapped wing and crew
Fighting-cock-fashion,—they had filched a pearl   1211
From dung-heap, and might boast with cause enough !
I was defrauded of all bargained for :
You know, the Pope knows, not a soul but knows
My dowry was derision, my gain—muck,   1215
My wife, (the Church declared my flesh and blood)
The nameless bastard of a common whore :
My old name turned henceforth to . . . shall I say
" He that received the ordure in his face? "
And they who planned this wrong, performed this wrong,
And then revealed this wrong to the wide world,   1221

Rounded myself in the ears with my own wrong,—
Why, these were (note hell's lucky malice, now!)
These were just they who, they alone, could act
And publish and proclaim their infamy,   1225
Secure that men would in a breath believe
Compassionate and pardon them,—for why?
They plainly were too stupid to invent,
Too simple to distinguish wrong from right,—
Inconscious agents they, the silly-sooth,   1230
Of heaven's retributive justice on the strong
Proud cunning violent oppressor—me!
Follow them to their fate and help your best,
You Rome, Arezzo, foes called friends of me,
They gave the good long laugh to, at my cost! 1235
Defray your share o' the cost, since you partook
The entertainment!   Do!—assured the while,
That not one stab, I dealt to right and left,
But went the deeper for a fancy—this—
That each might do me two-fold service, find   1240
A friend's face at the bottom of each wound,
And scratch its smirk a little!

                              Panciatichi!

There's a report at Florence,—is it true?—
That when your relative the Cardinal   1245
Built, only the other day, that barrack-bulk,
The palace in Via Larga, someone picked

From out the street a saucy quip enough
That fell there from its day's flight through the town,
About the flat front and the windows wide   1250
And bulging heap of cornice,—hitched the joke
Into a sonnet, signed his name thereto,
And forthwith pinned on post the pleasantry:
For which he's at the galleys, rowing now
Up to his waist in water,—just because   1255
Panciatic and *lymphatic* rhymed so pat!
I hope, Sir, those who passed this joke on me
Were not unduly punished? What say you,
Prince of the Church, my patron? Nay, indeed,
I shall not dare insult your wits so much   1260
As think this problem difficult to solve.
This Pietro and Violante then, I say,
These two ambiguous insects, changing name
And nature with the season's warmth or chill,—
Now, grovelled, grubbing toiling moiling ants,   1265
A very synonym of thrift and peace,—
Anon, with lusty June to prick their heart,
Soared i' the air, winged flies for more offence,
Circled me, buzzed me deaf and stung me blind,
And stunk me dead with fetor in the face   1270
Until I stopped the nuisance: there's my crime!
Pity I did not suffer them subside
Into some further shape and final form.

Of execrable life? My masters, no!
I, by one blow, wisely cut short at once   1275
Them and their transformations of disgust,
In the snug little Villa out of hand.
" Grant me confession, give bare time for that! "—
Shouted the sinner till his mouth was stopped.
His life confessed !—that was enough for me,   1280
Who came to see that he did penance.   'S death!
Here 's a coil raised, a pother and for what?
Because strength, being provoked by weakness, fought
And conquered,—the world never heard the like!
Pah, how I spend my breath on them, as if   1285
'T was their fate troubled me, too hard to range
Among the right and fit and proper things!

Ay, but Pompilia,—I await your word,—
She, unimpeached of crime, unimplicate
In folly, one of alien blood to these   1290
I punish, why extend my claim, exact
Her portion of the penalty?   Yes, friends,
I go too fast: the orator 's at fault:
Yes, ere I lay her, with your leave, by them
As she was laid at San Lorenzo late,   1295
I ought to step back, lead you by degrees,
Recounting at each step some fresh offence,
Up to the red bed,—never fear, I will!

Gaze at her, where I place her, to begin,
Confound me with her gentleness and worth !   1300
The horrible pair have fled and left her now,
She has her husband for her sole concern :
His wife, the woman fashioned for his help,
Flesh of his flesh, bone of his bone, the bride
To groom as is the Church and Spouse to Christ :
There she stands in his presence : " Thy desire   13c6
" Shall be to the husband, o'er thee shall he rule ! "
—" Pompilia, who declare that you love God,
" You know who said that : then, desire my love,
" Yield me contentment and be ruled aright ! "   1310
She sits up, she lies down, she comes and goes,
Kneels at the couch-side, overleans the sill
O' the window, cold and pale and mute as stone,
Strong as stone also.   " Well, are they not fled ?
" Am I not left, am I not one for all ?   1315
" Speak a word, drop a tear, detach a glance,
" Bless me or curse me of your own accord !
" Is it the ceiling only wants your soul,
" Is worth your eyes ? "   And then the eyes descend,
And do look at me.   Is it at the meal ?   1320
" Speak ! " she obeys, " Be silent ! " she obeys,
Counting the minutes till I cry " Depart,"
As brood-bird when you saunter past her eggs.
Departs she ? just the same through door and wall

I see the same stone strength of white despair.　1325
And all this will be never otherwise !
Before, the parents' presence lent her life :
She could play off her sex's armoury,
Entreat, reproach, be female to my male,
Try all the shrieking doubles of the hare,　1330
Go clamour to the Commissary, bid
The Archbishop hold my hands and stop my tongue,
And yield fair sport so : but the tactics change,
The hare stands stock-still to enrage the hound !
Since that day when she learned she was no child　1335
Of those she thought her parents,—that their trick
Had tricked me whom she thought sole trickster late,—
Why, I suppose she said within herself
" Then, no more struggle for my parents' sake !
" And, for my own sake, why needs struggle be ? "　1340
But is there no third party to the pact ?
What of her husband's relish or dislike
For this new game of giving up the game,
This worst offence of not offending more ?
I 'll not believe but instinct wrought in this,　1345
Set her on to conceive and execute
The preferable plague : how sure they probe—
These jades, the sensitivest soft of man !
The long black hair was wound now in a wisp,
Crowned sorrow better than the wild web late :　1350

No more soiled dress, 't is trimness triumphs now,
For how should malice go with negligence ?
The frayed silk looked the fresher for her spite !
There was an end to springing out of bed,
Praying me, with face buried on my feet,   1355
Be hindered of my pastime,— so an end
To my rejoinder, " What, on the ground at last ?
' Vanquished in fight, a supplicant for life ?
" What if I raise you ?   'Ware the casting down
" When next you fight me ! "   Then, she lay there,
        mine :
Now, mine she is if I please wring her neck,—   1361
A moment of disquiet, working eyes,
Protruding tongue, a long sigh, then no more,—
As if one killed the horse one could not ride !
Had I enjoined " Cut off the hair ! "—why, snap 1365
The scissors, and at once a yard or so
Had fluttered in black serpents to the floor :
But till I did enjoin it, how she combs,
Uncurls and draws out to the complete length,
Plaits, places the insulting rope on head   1370
To be an eyesore past dishevelment !
Is all done?   Then sit still again and stare !
I advise—no one think to bear that look
Of steady wrong, endured as steadily
—Through what sustainment of deluding hope? 1375

Who is the friend i' the background that notes all?
Who may come presently and close accounts?
This self-possession to the uttermost,
How does it differ in aught, save degree,
From the terrible patience of God? 1380
                              " All which just means,
" She did not love you ! "   Again the word is launched
And the fact fronts me !   What, you try the wards
With the true key and the dead lock flies ope?
No, it sticks fast and leaves you fumbling still ! 1385
You have some fifty servants, Cardinal,—
Which of them loves you ?   Which subordinate
But makes parade of such officiousness
That,—if there 's no love prompts it,—love, the sham,
Does twice the service done by love, the true ? 1390
God bless us liars, where 's one touch of truth
In what we tell the world, or world tells us,
Of how we love each other?   All the same,
We calculate on word and deed, nor err,—
Bid such a man do such a loving act, 1395
Sure of effect and negligent of cause,
Just as we bid a horse, with cluck of tongue,
Stretch his legs arch-wise, crouch his saddled back
To foot-reach of the stirrup—all for love,
And some for memory of the smart of switch 1400
On the inside of the foreleg—what care we?

Yet where's the bond obliges horse to man
Like that which binds fast wife to husband?   God
Laid down the law : gave man the brawny arm
And ball of fist—woman the beardless cheek   1405
And proper place to suffer in the side :
Since it is he can strike, let her obey !
Can she feel no love?   Let her show the more,
Sham the worse, damn herself praiseworthily !
Who's that soprano, Rome went mad about   1410
Last week while I lay rotting in my straw?
The very jailer gossiped in his praise—
How,—dressed up like Armida, though a man ;
And painted to look pretty, though a fright,—
He still made love so that the ladies swooned,   1415
Being an eunuch.   "Ah, Rinaldo mine !
" But to breathe by thee while Jove slays us both !
All the poor bloodless creature never felt,
Si, da, re, mi, fa, squeak and squall—for what?
Two gold zecchines the evening.   Here's my slave,
Whose body and soul depend upon my nod,   1421
Can't falter out the first note in the scale
For her life !   Why blame me if I take the life?
All women cannot give men love, forsooth !
No, nor all pullets lay the henwife eggs—   1425
Whereat she bids them remedy the fault,
Brood on a chalk-ball : soon the nest is stocked—

Otherwise, to the plucking and the spit !
This wife of mine was of another mood—
Would not begin the lie that ends with truth,   1430
Nor feign the love that brings real love about :
Wherefore I judged, sentenced and punished her.
But why particularize, defend the deed?
Say that I hated her for no one cause
Beyond my pleasure so to do,—what then ?   1435
Just on as much incitement acts the world,
All of you ! Look and like ! You favour one,
Browbeat another, leave alone a third,—
Why should you master natural caprice ?
Pure nature ! Try : plant elm by ash in file ;   1440
Both unexceptionable trees enough,
They ought to overlean each other, pair
At top, and arch across the avenue
The whole path to the pleasaunce : do they so—
Or loathe, lie off abhorrent each from each?   1445
Lay the fault elsewhere : since we must have faults,
Mine shall have been,—seeing there's ill in the end
Come of my course,—that I fare somehow worse
For the way I took : my fault . . . as God's my judge,
I see not where my fault lies, that's the truth !   1450
I ought . . . oh, ought in my own interest
Have let the whole adventure go untried,
This chance by marriage : or else, trying it,

Ought to have turned it to account, some one
O' the hundred otherwises?   Ay, my friend,   1455
Easy to say, easy to do: step right
Now you 've stepped left and stumbled on the thing,
—The red thing!   Doubt I any more than you
That practice makes man perfect?   Give again
The chance,—same marriage and no other wife, 1460
Be sure I 'll edify you!   That 's because
I 'm practised, grown fit guide for Guido's self.
You proffered guidance,—I know, none so well,—
You laid down law and rolled decorum out,
From pulpit-corner on the gospel-side,—   1465
Wanted to make your great experience mine,
Save me the personal search and pains so: thanks!
Take your word on life's use?   When I take his—
The muzzled ox that treadeth out the corn,
Gone blind in padding round and round one path,—
As to the taste of green grass in the field!   1471
What do you know o' the world that 's trodden flat
And salted sterile with your daily dung,
Leavened into a lump of loathsomeness?
Take your opinion of the modes of life,   1475
The aims of life, life's triumph or defeat,
How to feel, how to scheme, and how to do
Or else leave undone?   You preached long and loud
On high-days, " Take our doctrine upon trust!   1479

" Into the mill-house with you ! Grind our corn,
" Relish our chaff, and let the green grass grow ! "
I tried chaff, found I famished on such fare,
So made this mad rush at the mill-house-door,
Buried my head up to the ears in dew,
Browsed on the best : for which you brain me, Sirs !
Be it so. I conceived of life that way,   1486
And still declare—life, without absolute use
Of the actual sweet therein, is death, not life.
Give me,—pay down,—not promise, which is air,—
Something that 's out of life and better still,   1490
Make sure reward, make certain punishment,
Entice me, scare me,—I 'll forgo this life ;
Otherwise, no !—the less that words, mere wind,
Would cheat me of some minutes while they plague,
Baulk fulness of revenge here,—blame yourselves 1495
For this eruption of the pent-up soul
You prisoned first and played with afterward !
" Deny myself " meant simply pleasure you,
The sacred and superior, save the mark !
You,—whose stupidity and insolence   1500
I must defer to, soothe at every turn,—
Whose swine-like snuffling greed and grunting lust
I had to wink at or help gratify,—
While the same passions,—dared they perk in me,
Me, the immeasurably marked, by God,   1505

Master of the whole world of such as you,—
I, boast such passions? 'T was "Suppress them straight !
"Or stay, we 'll pick and choose before destroy.
" Here's wrath in you, a serviceable sword,—
" Beat it into a ploughshare ! What's this long   1510
" Lance-like ambition? Forge a pruning-hook,
" May be of service when our vines grow tall !
"But—sword use swordwise, spear thrust out as spear?
" Anathema ! Suppression is the word ! "
My nature, when the outrage was too gross,   1515
Widened itself an outlet over-wide
By way of answer, sought its own relief
With more of fire and brimstone than you wished.
All your own doing : preachers, blame yourselves !

'T is I preach while the hour-glass runs and runs ! 1520
God keep me patient ! All I say just means—
My wife proved, whether by her fault or mine,—
That's immaterial,—a true stumbling-block
I' the way of me her husband. I but plied
The hatchet yourselves use to clear a path,   1525
Was politic, played the game you warrant wins,
Plucked at law's robe a-rustle through the courts,
Bowed down to kiss divinity's buckled shoe
Cushioned i' the church : efforts all wide the aim !
Procedures to no purpose ! Then flashed truth.   1530

The letter kills, the spirit keeps alive
In law and gospel : there be nods and winks
Instruct a wise man to assist himself
In certain matters, nor seek aid at all.
" Ask money of me,"—quoth the clownish saw,—   1535
" And take my purse !   But,—speaking with respect,—
" Need you a solace for the troubled nose?
" Let everybody wipe his own himself ! "
Sirs, tell me free and fair !   Had things gone well
At the wayside inn : had I surprised asleep   1540
The runaways, as was so probable,
And pinned them each to other partridge-wise,
Through back and breast to breast and back, then bade
Bystanders witness if the spit, my sword,
Were loaded with unlawful game for once—   1545
Would you have interposed to damp the glow
Applauding me on every husband's cheek?
Would you have checked the cry "A judgment, see !
" A warning, note !   Be henceforth chaste, ye wives,
" Nor stray beyond your proper precinct, priests ! " 1550
If you had, then your house against itself
Divides, nor stands your kingdom any more.
Oh why, why was it not ordained just so ?
Why fell not things out so nor otherwise?
Ask that particular devil whose task it is   1555
To trip the all-but-at perfection,—slur

x.   P

The line of the painter just where paint leaves off
And life begins,—put ice into the ode
O' the poet while he cries " Next stanza—fire ! "
Inscribe all human effort with one word,   1560
Artistry's haunting curse, the Incomplete !
Being incomplete, my act escaped success.
Easy to blame now !   Every fool can swear
To hole in net that held and slipped the fish.
But, treat my act with fair unjaundiced eye,   1565
What was there wanting to a masterpiece
Except the luck that lies beyond a man ?
My way with the woman, now proved grossly wrong,
Just missed of being gravely grandly right
And making mouths laugh on the other side.   1570
Do, for the poor obstructed artist's sake,
Go with him over that spoiled work once more !
Take only its first flower, the ended act
Now in the dusty pod, dry and defunct !
I march to the Villa, and my men with me,   1575
That evening, and we reach the door and stand.
I say . . . no, it shoots through me lightning-like
While I pause, breathe, my hand upon the latch,
" Let me forebode !   Thus far, too much success :
" I want the natural failure—find it where?   1580
" Which thread will have to break and leave a loop
" I' the meshy combination, my brain's loom

" Wove this long while, and now next minute tests?
" Of three that are to catch, two should go free,
" One must : all three surprised,—impossible !   1585
" Beside, I seek three and may chance on six,—
" This neighbour, t' other gossip,—the babe's birth
" Brings such to fireside, and folks give them wine,—
" 'T is late : but when I break in presently
" One will be found outlingering the rest   1590
" For promise of a posset,—one whose shout
" Would raise the dead down in the catacombs,
" Much more the city-watch that goes its round.
" When did I ever turn adroitly up
" To sun some brick embedded in the soil,   1595
" And with one blow crush all three scorpions there ?
" Or Pietro or Violante shambles off—
" It cannot be but I surprise my wife—
" If only she is stopped and stamped on, good !
" That shall suffice : more is improbable.   1600
" Now I may knock ! "   And this once for my sake
The impossible was effected : I called king,
Queen and knave in a sequence, and cards came,
All three, three only !   So, I had my way,
Did my deed : so, unbrokenly lay bare   1605
Each tænia that had sucked me dry of juice,
At last outside me, not an inch of ring
Left now to writhe about and root itself

I' the heart all powerless for revenge ! Henceforth
I might thrive : these were drawn and dead and damned.
Oh Cardinal, the deep long sigh you heave   1611
When the load 's off you, ringing as it runs
All the way down the serpent-stair to hell !
No doubt the fine delirium flustered me,
Turned my brain with the influx of success   1615
As if the sole need now were to wave wand
And find doors fly wide,—wish and have my will,—
The rest o' the scheme would care for itself : escape
Easy enough were that, and poor beside !
It all but proved so,—ought to quite have proved,   1620
Since, half the chances had sufficed, set free
Anyone, with his senses at command,
From thrice the danger of my flight.   But, drunk,
Redundantly triumphant,—some reverse
Was sure to follow !   There 's no other way   1625
Accounts for such prompt perfect failure then
And there on the instant.   Any day o' the week,
A ducat slid discreetly into palm
O' the mute post-master, while you whisper him—
How you the Count and certain four your knaves,   1630
Have just been mauling who was malapert,
Suspect the kindred may prove troublesome,
Therefore, want horses in a hurry,— that
And nothing more secures you any day

The pick o' the stable! Yet I try the trick, 1635
Double the bribe, call myself Duke for Count,
And say the dead man only was a Jew,
And for my pains find I am dealing just
With the one scrupulous fellow in all Rome—
Just this immaculate official stares, 1640
Sees I want hat on head and sword in sheath,
Am splashed with other sort of wet than wine,
Shrugs shoulder, puts my hand by, gold and all,
Stands on the strictness of the rule o' the road!
"Where's the Permission?" Where's the wretched rag
With the due seal and sign of Rome's Police, 1646
To be had for asking, half-an-hour ago?
"Gone? Get another, or no horses hence!"
He dares not stop me, we five glare too grim,
But hinders,—hacks and hamstrings sure enough, 1650
Gives me some twenty miles of miry road
More to march in the middle of that night
Whereof the rough beginning taxed the strength
O' the youngsters, much more mine, both soul and flesh,
Who had to think as well as act: dead-beat, 1655
We gave in ere we reached the boundary
And safe spot out of this irrational Rome,—
Where, on dismounting from our steeds next day,
We had snapped our fingers at you, safe and sound,
Tuscans once more in blessed Tuscany, 1660

Where laws make wise allowance, understand
Civilized life and do its champions right !
Witness the sentence of the Rota there,
Arezzo uttered, the Granduke confirmed,
One week before I acted on its hint,—   1665
Giving friend Guillichini, for his love,
The galleys, and my wife your saint, Rome's saint,—
Rome manufactures saints enough to know,—
Seclusion at the Stinche for her life.
All this, that all but was, might all have been,   1670
Yet was not ! baulked by just a scrupulous knave
Whose palm was horn through handling horses' hoofs
And could not close upon my proffered gold !
What say you to the spite of fortune ? Well,
The worst 's in store : thus hindered, haled this way
To Rome again by hangdogs, whom find I   1676
Here, still to fight with, but my pale frail wife ?
—Riddled with wounds by one not like to waste
The blows he dealt,—knowing anatomy,—
(I think I told you) bound to pick and choose   1680
The vital parts ! 'T was learning all in vain !
She too must shimmer through the gloom o' the grave,
Come and confront me—not at judgment-seat
Where I could twist her soul, as erst her flesh,
And turn her truth into a lie,—but there,   1685
O' the death-bed, with God's hand between us both,

Striking me dumb, and helping her to speak,
Tell her own story her own way, and turn
My plausibility to nothingness !
Four whole days did Pompilia keep alive,   1690
With the best surgery of Rome agape
At the miracle,—this cut, the other slash,
And yet the life refusing to dislodge,
Four whole extravagant impossible days,
Till she had time to finish and persuade   1695
Every man, every woman, every child
In Rome, of what she would : the selfsame she
Who, but a year ago, had wrung her hands,
Reddened her eyes and beat her breasts, rehearsed
The whole game at Arezzo, nor availed   1700
Thereby to move one heart or raise one hand !
When destiny intends you cards like these,
What good of skill and preconcerted play ?
Had she been found dead, as I left her dead,
I should have told a tale brooked no reply :   1705
You scarcely will suppose me found at fault
With that advantage ! " What brings me to Rome ?
" Necessity to claim and take my wife :
" Better, to claim and take my new-born babe,—
" Strong in paternity a fortnight old,   1710
" When 't is at strongest : warily I work,
" Knowing the machinations of my foe ;

" I have companionship and use the night :
" I seek my wife and child,—I find—no child
" But wife, in the embraces of that priest   1715
" Who caused her to elope from me.   These two,
" Backed by the pander-pair who watch the while,
" Spring on me like so many tiger-cats,
" Glad of the chance to end the intruder.   I—
" What should I do but stand on my defence,   1720
" Strike right, strike left, strike thick and threefold, slay,
" Not all—because the coward priest escapes.
" Last, I escape, in fear of evil tongues,
" And having had my taste of Roman law."
What 's disputable, refutable here ?—   1725
Save by just this one ghost-thing half on earth,
Half out of it,—as if she held God's hand
While she leant back and looked her last at me,
Forgiving me (here monks begin to weep)
Oh, from her very soul, commending mine   1730
To heavenly mercies which are infinite,—
While fixing fast my head beneath your knife !
'T is fate not fortune.   All is of a piece !
When was it chance informed me of my youths ?
My rustic four o' the family, soft swains,   1735
What sweet surprise had they in store for me,
Those of my very household,—what did Law
Twist with her rack-and-cord-contrivance late

From out their bones and marrow ? What but this—
Had no one of these several stumbling-blocks   1740
Stopped me, they yet were cherishing a scheme,
All of their honest country homespun wit,
To quietly next day at crow of cock
Cut my own throat too, for their own behoof,
Seeing I had forgot to clear accounts   1745
O' the instant, nowise slackened speed for that,—
And somehow never might find memory,
Once safe back in Arezzo, where things change,
And a court-lord needs mind no country lout.
Well, being the arch-offender, I die last,—   1750 .
May, ere my head falls, have my eyesight free,
Nor miss them dangling high on either hand,
Like scarecrows in a hemp-field, for their pains !

And then my Trial,—'t is my Trial that bites
Like a corrosive, so the cards are packed,   1755
Dice loaded, and my life-stake tricked away !
Look at my lawyers, lacked they grace of law,
Latin or logic ? Were not they fools to the height,
Fools to the depth, fools to the level between,
O' the foolishness set to decide the case ?   1760
They feign, they flatter; nowise does it skill,
Everything goes against me : deal each judge
His dole of flattery and feigning,—why,

He turns and tries and snuffs and savours it,
As some old fly the sugar-grain, your gift;   1765
Then eyes your thumb and finger, brushes clean
The absurd old head of him, and whisks away,
Leaving your thumb and finger dirty.   Faugh!

And finally, after this long-drawn range
Of affront and failure, failure and affront,—   1770
This path, 'twixt crosses leading to a skull,
Paced by me barefoot, bloodied by my palms
From the entry to the end,—there's light at length,
A cranny of escape: appeal may be
To the old man, to the father, to the Pope,   1775
For a little life—from one whose life is spent,
A little pity—from pity's source and seat,
A little indulgence to rank, privilege,
From one who is the thing personified,
Rank, privilege, indulgence, grown beyond   1780
Earth's bearing, even, ask Jansenius else!
Still the same answer, still no other tune
From the cicala perched at the tree-top
Than crickets noisy round the root: 't is " Die!"
Bids Law—" Be damned! " adds Gospel,—nay,   1785
No word so frank,—'t is rather, " Save yourself! "
The Pope subjoins—" Confess and be absolved!
"So shall my credit countervail your shame,

" And the world see I have not lost the knack
" Of trying all the spirits : yours, my son,   1790
" Wants but a fiery washing to emerge
" In clarity !   Come, cleanse you, ease the ache
" Of these old bones, refresh our bowels, boy ! "
Do I mistake your mission from the Pope ?
Then, bear his Holiness the mind of me !   1795
I do get strength from being thrust to wall,
Successively wrenched from pillar and from post
By this tenacious hate of fortune, hate
Of all things in, under, and above earth.
Warfare, begun this mean unmanly mode,   1800
Does best to end so,—gives earth spectacle
Of a brave fighter who succumbs to odds
That turn defeat to victory.   Stab, I fold
My mantle round me !   Rome approves my act :
Applauds the blow which costs me life but keeps 1805
My honour spotless : Rome would praise no more
Had I fallen, say, some fifteen years ago,
Helping Vienna when our Aretines
Flocked to Duke Charles and fought Turk Mustafa ;
Nor would you two be trembling o'er my corpse 1810
With all this exquisite solicitude.
Why is it that I make such suit to live ?
The popular sympathy that 's round me now
Would break like bubble that o'er-domes a fly :

Solid enough while he lies quiet there,   1815
But let him want the air and ply the wing,
Why, it breaks and bespatters him, what else?
Cardinal, if the Pope had pardoned me,
And I walked out of prison through the crowd,
It would not be your arm I should dare press!   1820
Then, if I got safe to my place again,
How sad and sapless were the years to come!
I go my old ways and find things grown grey;
You priests leer at me, old friends look askance,
The mob 's in love, I 'll wager, to a man,   1825
With my poor young good beauteous murdered wife:
For hearts require instruction how to beat,
And eyes, on warrant of the story, wax
Wanton at portraiture in white and black
Of dead Pompilia gracing ballad-sheet,   1830
Which eyes, lived she unmurdered and unsung,
Would never turn though she paced street as bare
As the mad penitent ladies do in France.
My brothers quietly would edge me out
Of use and management of things called mine;   1835
Do I command? " You stretched command before!"
Show anger? " Anger little helped you once!"
Advise? " How managed you affairs of old?"
My very mother, all the while they gird,
Turns eye up, gives confirmatory groan;   1840

For unsuccess, explain it how you will,
Disqualifies you, makes you doubt yourself,
—Much more, is found decisive by your friends.
Beside, am I not fifty years of age?   1844
What new leap would a life take, checked like mine
I' the spring at outset? Where's my second chance?
Ay, but the babe . . . I had forgot my son,
My heir! Now for a burst of gratitude!
There 's some appropriate service to intone,
Some *gaudeamus* and thanksgiving-psalm!   1850
Old, I renew my youth in him, and poor
Possess a treasure,—is not that the phrase?
Only I must wait patient twenty years—
Nourishing all the while, as father ought,
The excrescence with my daily blood of life.   1855
Does it respond to hope, such sacrifice,—
Grows the wen plump while I myself grow lean?
Why, here 's my son and heir in evidence,
Who stronger, wiser, handsomer than I
By fifty years, relieves me of each load,—   1860
Tames my hot horse, carries my heavy gun,
Courts my coy mistress,—has his apt advice
On house-economy, expenditure,
And what not. All which good gifts and great growth
Because of my decline, he brings to bear   1865
On Guido, but half apprehensive how

He cumbers earth, crosses the brisk young Count,
Who civilly would thrust him from the scene.
Contrariwise, does the blood-offering fail?
There 's an ineptitude, one blank the more   1870
Added to earth in semblance of my child?
Then, this has been a costly piece of work,
My life exchanged for his!—why he, not I,
Enjoy the world, if no more grace accrue?
Dwarf me, what giant have you made of him?   1875
I do not dread the disobedient son:
I know how to suppress rebellion there,
Being not quite the fool my father was.
But grant the medium measure of a man,
The usual compromise 'twixt fool and sage,   1880
—You know—the tolerably-obstinate,
The not-so-much-perverse but you may train,
The true son-servant that, when parent bids
" Go work, son, in my vineyard!" makes reply
" I go, Sir!"—Why, what profit in your son   1885
Beyond the drudges you might subsidize,
Have the same work from, at a paul the head?
Look at those four young precious olive-plants
Reared at Vittiano,—not on flesh and blood,
These twenty years, but black bread and sour wine!
I bade them put forth tender branch, hook, hold, 1891
And hurt three enemies I had in Rome:

They did my hest as unreluctantly,
At promise of a dollar, as a son
Adjured by mumping memories of the past.   1895
No, nothing repays youth expended so—
Youth, I say, who am young still : grant but leave
To live my life out, to the last I 'd live
And die conceding age no right of youth !
It is the will runs the renewing nerve   1900
Through flaccid flesh that faints before the time.
Therefore no sort of use for son have I—
Sick, not of life's feast but of steps to climb
To the house where life prepares her feast, — of means
To the end : for make the end attainable   1905
Without the means,—my relish were like yours.
A man may have an appetite enough
For a whole dish of robins ready cooked,
And yet lack courage to face sleet, pad snow,
And snare sufficiently for supper.   1910

      Thus
The time 's arrived when, ancient Roman-like,
I am bound to fall on my own sword : why not
Say—Tuscan-like, more ancient, better still ?
Will you hear truth can do no harm nor good ?   1915
I think I never was at any time
A Christian, as you nickname all the world.

Me among others : truce to nonsense now !
Name me, a primitive religionist—
As should the aboriginary be   1920
I boast myself, Etruscan, Aretine,
One sprung,—your frigid Virgil's fieriest word,—
From fauns and nymphs, trunks and the heart of oak,
With,—for a visible divinity,—
The portent of a Jove Ægiochus   1925
Descried 'mid clouds, lightning and thunder, couched
On topmost crag of your Capitoline :
'T is in the Seventh Æneid,—what, the Eighth ?
Right,—thanks, Abate,—though the Christian 's dumb,
The Latinist 's vivacious in you yet !   1930
I know my grandsire had our tapestry
Marked with the motto, 'neath a certain shield,
Whereto his grandson presently will give gules
To vary azure.   First we fight for faiths,
But get to shake hands at the last of all :   1935
Mine 's your faith too,—in Jove Ægiochus !
Nor do Greek gods, that serve as supplement,
Jar with the simpler scheme, if understood.
We want such intermediary race
To make communication possible ;   1940
The real thing were too lofty, we too low,
Midway hang these : we feel their use so plain
In linking height to depth, that we doff hat

And put no question nor pry narrowly
Into the nature hid behind the names.   1945
We grudge no rite the fancy may demand;
But never, more than needs, invent, refine,
Improve upon requirement, idly wise
Beyond the letter, teaching gods their trade,
Which is to teach us: we'll obey when taught. 1950
Why should we do our duty past the need?
When the sky darkens, Jove is wroth,—say prayer!
When the sun shines and Jove is glad,—sing psalm!
But wherefore pass prescription and devise
Blood-offering for sweat-service, lend the rod 1955
A pungency through pickle of our own?
Learned Abate,—no one teaches you
What Venus means and who's Apollo here!
I spare you, Cardinal,—but, though you wince,
You know me, I know you, and both know that!
So, if Apollo bids us fast, we fast: 1961
But where does Venus order we stop sense
When Master Pietro rhymes a pleasantry?
Give alms prescribed on Friday: but, hold hand
Because your foe lies prostrate,—where's the word
Explicit in the book debars revenge?   1966
The rationale of your scheme is just
" Pay toll here, there pursue your pleasure free!"
So do you turn to use the medium-powers,

X.   Q

Mars and Minerva, Bacchus and the rest,   1970
And so are saved propitiating—whom ?
What all-good, all-wise and all-potent Jove
Vexed by the very sins in man, himself
Made life's necessity when man he made ?
Irrational bunglers ! So, the living truth   1975
Revealed to strike Pan dead, ducks low at last,
Prays leave to hold its own and live good days
Provided it go masque grotesquely, called
Christian not Pagan.   Oh, you purged the sky
Of all gods save the One, the great and good,   1980
Clapped hands and triumphed ! But the change came
          fast :
The inexorable need in man for life—
(Life, you may mulct and minish to a grain
Out of the lump, so that the grain but live)
Laughed at your substituting death for life,   1985
And bade you do your worst : which worst was done
In just that age styled primitive and pure
When Saint this, Saint that, dutifully starved,
Froze, fought with beasts, was beaten and abused
And finally ridded of his flesh by fire :   1990
He kept life-long unspotted from the world !
Next age, how goes the game, what mortal gives
His life and emulates Saint that, Saint this?
Men mutter, make excuse or mutiny,

In fine are minded all to leave the new,   1995
Stick to the old,—enjoy old liberty,
No prejudice in enjoyment, if you please,
To the new profession : sin o' the sly, henceforth !
The law stands though the letter kills : what then ?
The spirit saves as unmistakeably.   2000
Omniscience sees, Omnipotence could stop,
Omnibenevolence pardons : it must be,
Frown law its fiercest, there 's a wink somewhere !

Such was the logic in this head of mine :
I, like the rest, wrote " poison " on my bread,   2005
But broke and ate :—said "Those that use the sword
"Shall perish by the same ;" then stabbed my foe.
I stand on solid earth, not empty air :
Dislodge me, let your Pope's crook hale me hence !
Not he, nor you !   And I so pity both,   2010
I 'll make the true charge you want wit to make :
" Count Guido, who reveal our mystery,
" And trace all issues to the love of life.
" We having life to love and guard, like you,
" Why did you put us upon self-defence?   2015
" You well knew what prompt pass-word would appease
" The sentry's ire when folk infringed his bounds,
" And yet kept mouth shut : do you wonder then
" If, in mere decency, he shot you dead?

" He can't have people play such pranks as yours 2020
" Beneath his nose at noonday : you disdained
" To give him an excuse before the world
" By crying ' I break rule to save our camp ! '
" Under the old rule, such offence were death ;
" And you had heard the Pontifex pronounce   2025
" ' Since you slay foe and violate the form,
" ' Slaying turns murder, which were sacrifice
" ' Had you, while, say, law-suiting foe to death,
" ' But raised an altar to the Unknown God
" ' Or else the Genius of the Vatican.'   2030
" Why then this pother?—all because the Pope,
" Doing his duty, cried ' A foreigner,
" ' You scandalize the natives : here at Rome
" ' *Romano vivitur more:* wise men, here,
" ' Put the Church forward and efface themselves. 2035
" ' The fit defence had been,—you stamped on wheat,
" ' Intending all the time to trample tares,—
" ' Were fain extirpate, then, the heretic,
" ' You now find, in your haste was slain a fool :
" ' Nor Pietro, nor Violante, nor your wife   2040
" ' Meant to breed up your babe a Molinist !
" ' Whence you are duly contrite.   Not one word
" ' Of all this wisdom did you urge : which slip
" ' Death must atone for.' "

                    So, let death atone ! 2045

So ends mistake, so end mistakers!—end
Perhaps to recommence,—how should I know?
Only, be sure, no punishment, no pain
Childish, preposterous, impossible,
But some such fate as Ovid could foresee,—   2050
Byblis in fluvium, let the weak soul end
In water, *sed Lycaon in lupum*, but
The strong become a wolf for evermore!
Change that Pompilia to a puny stream
Fit to reflect the daisies on its bank!   2055
Let me turn wolf, be whole, and sate, for once,—
Wallow in what is now a wolfishness
Coerced too much by the humanity
That's half of me as well! Grow out of man,
Glut the wolf-nature,—what remains but grow   2060
Into the man again, be man indeed
And all man? Do I ring the changes right?
Deformed, transformed, reformed, informed, conformed!
The honest instinct, pent and crossed through life,
Let surge by death into a visible flow   2065
Of rapture: as the strangled thread of flame
Painfully winds, annoying and annoyed,
Malignant and maligned, thro' stone and ore,
Till earth exclude the stranger: vented once,
It finds full play, is recognized a-top   2070
Some mountain as no such abnormal birth,

Fire for the mount, not streamlet for the vale !
Ay, of the water was that wife of mine—
Be it for good, be it for ill, no run
O' the red thread through that insignificance !　2075
Again, how she is at me with those eyes !
Away with the empty stare ! Be holy still,
And stupid ever ! Occupy your patch
Of private snow that 's somewhere in what world
May now be growing icy round your head,　2080
And aguish at your foot-print,—freeze not me,
Dare follow not another step I take,
Not with so much as those detested eyes,
No, though they follow but to pray me pause
On the incline, earth's edge that 's next to hell !　2085
None of your abnegation of revenge !
Fly at me frank, tug while I tear again !
There 's God, go tell Him, testify your worst !
Not she ! There was no touch in her of hate :
And it would prove her hell, if I reached mine !　2090
To know I suffered, would still sadden her,
Do what the angels might to make amends !
Therefore there 's either no such place as hell,
Or thence shall I be thrust forth, for her sake,
And thereby undergo three hells, not one—　2095
1 who, with outlet for escape to heaven,
Would tarry if such flight allowed my foe

To raise his head, relieved of that firm foot
Had pinned him to the fiery pavement else!
So am I made, "who did not make myself:"   2100
(How dared she rob my own lip of the word?)
Beware me in what other world may be!—
Pompilia, who have brought me to this pass!
All I know here, will I say there, and go
Beyond the saying with the deed. Some use   2105
There cannot but be for a mood like mine,
Implacable, persistent in revenge.
She maundered "All is over and at end:
"I go my own road, go you where God will!
"Forgive you? I forget you!" There's the saint
That takes your taste, you other kind of men!   2111
How you had loved her! Guido wanted skill
To value such a woman at her worth!
Properly the instructed criticize
"What's here, you simpleton have tossed to take   2115
"Its chance i' the gutter? This a daub, indeed?
"Why, 't is a Rafael that you kicked to rags!"
Perhaps so: some prefer the pure design:
Give me my gorge of colour, glut of gold
In a glory round the Virgin made for me!   2120
Titian's the man, not Monk Angelico
Who traces you some timid chalky ghost
That turns the church into a charnel: ay,

Just such a pencil might depict my wife!
She,—since she, also, would not change herself,— 2125
Why could not she come in some heart-shaped cloud,
Rainbowed about with riches, royalty
Rimming her round, as round the tintless lawn
Guardingly runs the selvage cloth of gold?
I would have left the faint fine gauze untouched,
Needle-worked over with its lily and rose,   2131
Let her bleach unmolested in the midst,
Chill that selected solitary spot
Of quietude she pleased to think was life.
Purity, pallor grace the lawn no doubt   2135
When there's the costly bordure to unthread
And make again an ingot : but what's grace
When you want meat and drink and clothes and fire?
A tale comes to my mind that's apposite—
Possibly true, probably false, a truth   2140
Such as all truths we live by, Cardinal!
'T is said, a certain ancestor of mine
Followed—whoever was the potentate,
To Paynimrie, and in some battle, broke
Through more than due allowance of the foe,   2145
And, risking much his own life, saved the lord's.
Battered and bruised, the Emperor scrambles up,
Rubs his eyes and looks round and sees my sire,
Picks a furze-sprig from out his hauberk-joint,

(Token how near the ground went majesty)   2150
And says " Take this, and if thou get safe home,
" Plant the same in thy garden-ground to grow :
" Run thence an hour in a straight line, and stop :
" Describe a circle round (for central point)
" The furze aforesaid, reaching every way   2155
" The length of that hour's run : I give it thee,—
" The central point, to build a castle there,
" The space circumjacent, for fit demesne,
" The whole to be thy children's heritage,—
" Whom, for thy sake, bid thou wear furze on cap ! "
Those are my arms : we turned the furze a tree   2161
To show more, and the greyhound tied thereto,
Straining to start, means swift and greedy both ;
He stands upon a triple mount of gold—
By Jove, then, he 's escaping from true gold   2165
And trying to arrive at empty air !
Aha ! the fancy never crossed my mind !
My father used to tell me, and subjoin   .
" As for the castle, that took wings and flew :
" The broad lands,—why, to traverse them to-day
" Scarce tasks my gouty feet, and in my prime   2171
" I doubt not I could stand and spit so far :
" But for the furze, boy, fear no lack of that,
" So long as fortune leaves one field to grub !
" Wherefore, hurra for furze and loyalty ! "   2175

What may I mean, where may the lesson lurk?
" Do not bestow on man, by way of gift,
" Furze without land for framework,—vaunt no grace
" Of purity, no furze-sprig of a wife,
" To me, i' the thick of battle for my bread,   2180
" Without some better dowry,—gold will do ! "
No better gift than sordid muck?   Yes, Sirs !
Many more gifts much better.   Give them me !
O those Olimpias bold, those Biancas brave,   2184
That brought a husband power worth Ormuz' wealth !
Cried " Thou being mine, why, what but thine am I?
" Be thou to me law, right, wrong, heaven and hell !
" Let us blend souls, blent, thou in me, to bid
" Two bodies work one pleasure !   What are these   2189
" Called king, priest, father, mother, stranger, friend?
" They fret thee or they frustrate?   Give the word—
" Be certain they shall frustrate nothing more !
" And who is this young florid foolishness
" That holds thy fortune in his pigmy clutch,
" —Being a prince and potency, forsooth !—   2195
" He hesitates to let the trifle go?
" Let me but seal up eye, sing ear to sleep
" Sounder than Samson,—pounce thou on the prize
" Shall slip from off my breast, and down couch-
        side,
" And on to floor, and far as my lord's feet—   2200

" Where he stands in the shadow with the knife,

" Waiting to see what Delilah dares do !

" Is the youth fair ? What is a man to me

" Who am thy call-bird? Twist his neck—my
    dupe's,—

" Then take the breast shall turn a breast indeed ! "

Such women are there; and they marry whom ? 2206

Why, when a man has gone and hanged himself

Because of what he calls a wicked wife,—

See, if the very turpitude bemoaned

Prove not mere excellence the fool ignores !   2210

His monster is perfection,—Circe, sent

Straight from the sun, with wand the idiot blames

As not an honest distaff to spin wool !

O thou Lucrezia, is it long to wait

Yonder where all the gloom is in a glow   2215

With thy suspected presence?—virgin yet,

Virtuous again, in face of what 's to teach—

Sin unimagined, unimaginable,—

I come to claim my bride,—thy Borgia's self

Not half the burning bridegroom I shall be !   2220

Cardinal, take away your crucifix !

Abate, leave my lips alone,—they bite !

Vainly you try to change what should not change,

And shall not. I have bared, you bathe my heart—

It grows the stonier for your saving dew !   2225

You steep the substance, you would lubricate,
In waters that but touch to petrify !

You too are petrifactions of a kind :
Move not a muscle that shows mercy.   Rave
Another twelve hours, every word were waste !   2230
I thought you would not slay impenitence,
But teased, from men you slew, contrition first,—
I thought you had a conscience.   Cardinal,
You know I am wronged !—wronged, say, and wronged,
     maintain.
Was this strict inquisition made for blood   2235
When first you showed us scarlet on your back,
Called to the College?   Your straightforward way
To your legitimate end,—I think it passed
Over a scantling of heads brained, hearts broke,
Lives trodden into dust !   How otherwise ?   2240
Such was the way o' the world, and so you walked.
Does memory haunt your pillow?   Not a whit.
God wills you never pace your garden-path,
One appetizing hour ere dinner-time,
But your intrusion there treads out of life   2245
A universe of happy innocent things :
Feel you remorse about that damsel-fly
Which buzzed so near your mouth and flapped your face?
You blotted it from being at a blow :

It was a fly, you were a man, and more, 2250
Lord of created things, so took your course.
Manliness, mind,—these are things fit to save,
Fit to brush fly from : why, because I take
My course, must needs the Pope kill me?—kill you !
You! for this instrument, he throws away, 2255
Is strong to serve a master, and were yours
To have and hold and get much good from out !
The Pope who dooms me needs must die next year ;
I 'll tell you how the chances are supposed
For his successor : first the Chamberlain, 2260
Old San Cesario,—Colloredo, next,—
Then, one, two, three, four, I refuse to name ;
After these, comes Altieri ; then come you—
Seventh on the list you come, unless . . . ha, ha,
How can a dead hand give a friend a lift ? 2265
Are you the person to despise the help
O' the head shall drop in pannier presently?
So a child seesaws on or kicks away
The fulcrum-stone that 's all the sage requires
To fit his lever to and move the world. 2270
Cardinal, I adjure you in God's name,
Save my life, fall at the Pope's feet, set forth
Things your own fashion, not in words like these
Made for a sense like yours who apprehend !
Translate into the Court-conventional 2275

" Count Guido must not die, is innocent !
" Fair, be assured !   But what an he were foul,
" Blood-drenched and murder-crusted head to foot ?
" Spare one whose death insults the Emperor,
" Nay, outrages the Louis you so love !   2280
" He has friends who will avenge him ; enemies
" Who will hate God now with impunity,
" Missing the old coercive : would you send
" A soul straight to perdition, dying frank   2284
" An atheist ? "   Go and say this, for God's sake !
—Why, you don't think I hope you 'll say one word ?
Neither shall I persuade you from your stand
Nor you persuade me from my station : take
Your crucifix away, I tell you twice !

Come, I am tired of silence !   Pause enough !   2290
You have prayed : I have gone inside my soul
And shut its door behind me : 't is your torch
Makes the place dark : the darkness let alone
Grows tolerable twilight : one may grope
And get to guess at length and breadth and depth.
What is this fact I feel persuaded of—   2296
This something like a foothold in the sea,
Although Saint Peter's bark scuds, billow-borne,
Leaves me to founder where it flung me first ?
Spite of your splashing, I am high and dry !   2300

God takes his own part in each thing He made;
Made for a reason, He conserves his work,
Gives each its proper instinct of defence.
My lamblike wife could neither bark nor bite,
She bleated, bleated, till for pity pure   2305
The village roused up, ran with pole and prong
To the rescue, and behold the wolf's at bay!
Shall he try bleating?—or take turn or two,
Since the wolf owns some kinship with the fox,
And, failing to escape the foe by craft,   2310
Give up attempt, die fighting quietly?
The last bad blow that strikes fire in at eye
And on to brain, and so out, life and all,
How can it but be cheated of a pang
If, fighting quietly, the jaws enjoy   2315
One re-embrace in mid back-bone they break,
After their weary work thro' the foe's flesh?
That's the wolf-nature.   Don't mistake my trope!
A Cardinal so qualmish?   Eminence,
My fight is figurative, blows i' the air,   2320
Brain-war with powers and principalities,
Spirit-bravado, no real fisticuffs!
I shall not presently, when the knock comes,
Cling to this bench nor claw the hangman's face,
No, trust me!   I conceive worse lots than mine.
Whether it be, the old contagious fit   2326

And plague o' the prison have surprised me too,
The appropriate drunkenness of the death-hour
Crept on my sense, kind work o' the wine and myrrh,—
I know not,—I begin to taste my strength,   2330
Careless, gay even.   What's the worth of life?
The Pope's dead now, my murderous old man,
For Tozzi told me so: and you, forsooth—
Why, you don't think, Abate, do your best,
You'll live a year more with that hacking cough 2335
And blotch of crimson where the cheek's a pit?
Tozzi has got you also down in book!
Cardinal, only seventh of seventy near,
Is not one called Albano in the lot?
Go eat your heart, you'll never be a Pope!   2340
Inform me, is it true you left your love,
A Pucci, for promotion in the church?
She's more than in the church,—in the churchyard!
Plautilla Pucci, your affianced bride,
Has dust now in the eyes that held the love,—   2345
And Martinez, suppose they make you Pope,
Stops that with *veto*,—so, enjoy yourself!
I see you all reel to the rock, you waves—
Some forthright, some describe a sinuous track,
Some, crested brilliantly, with heads above,   2350
Some in a strangled swirl sunk who knows how,
But all bound whither the main-current sets,

Rockward, an end in foam for all of you !
What if I be o'ertaken, pushed to the front
By all you crowding smoother souls behind, 2355
And reach, a minute sooner than was meant,
The boundary whereon I break to mist ?
Go to ! the smoothest safest of you all,
Most perfect and compact wave in my train,
Spite of the blue tranquillity above, 2360
Spite of the breadth before of lapsing peace
Where broods the halcyon and the fish leaps free,
Will presently begin to feel the prick
At lazy heart, the push at torpid brain,
Will rock vertiginously in turn, and reel, 2365
And, emulative, rush to death like me.
Later or sooner by a minute then,
So much for the untimeliness of death !
And, as regards the manner that offends,
The rude and rough, I count the same for gain. 2370
Be the act harsh and quick ! Undoubtedly
The soul 's condensed and, twice itself, expands
To burst thro' life, by alternation due,
Into the other state whate'er it prove.
You never know what life means till you die : 2375
Even throughout life, 't is death that makes life live,
Gives it whatever the significance.
For see, on your own ground and argument,

X. R

Suppose life had no death to fear, how find
A possibility of nobleness   2380
In man, prevented daring any more?
What 's love, what 's faith without a worst to dread?
Lack-lustre jewelry! but faith and love
With death behind them bidding do or die—
Put such a foil at back, the sparkle 's born!   2385
From out myself how the strange colours come!
Is there a new rule in another world?
Be sure I shall resign myself: as here
I recognized no law I could not see,
There, what I see, I shall acknowledge too: 2390
On earth I never took the Pope for God,
In heaven I shall scarce take God for the Pope.
Unmanned, remanned: I hold it probable—
With something changeless at the heart of me
To know me by, some nucleus that 's myself: 2395
Accretions did it wrong? Away with them—
You soon shall see the use of fire!

                                    Till when,
All that was, is; and must forever be.
Nor is it in me to unhate my hates,—   2400
I use up my last strength to strike once more
Old Pietro in the wine-house-gossip-face,
To trample underfoot the whine and wile

Of beast Violante,—and I grow one gorge
To loathingly reject Pompilia's pale   2405
Poison my hasty hunger took for food.
A strong tree wants no wreaths about its trunk,
No cloying cups, no sickly sweet of scent,
But sustenance at root, a bucketful.
How else lived that Athenian who died so,   2410
Drinking hot bull's blood, fit for men like me?
I lived and died a man, and take man's chance,
Honest and bold : right will be done to such.

Who are these you have let descend my stair?
Ha, their accursed psalm !   Lights at the sill !   2415
Is it "Open" they dare bid you?   Treachery !
Sirs, have I spoken one word all this while
Out of the world of words I had to say?
Not one word !   All was folly—I laughed and mocked !
Sirs, my first true word, all truth and no lie,   2420
Is—save me notwithstanding !   Life is all !
I was just stark mad,—let the madman live
Pressed by as many chains as you please pile !
Don't open !   Hold me from them !   I am yours,
I am the Granduke's—no, I am the Pope's !   2425
Abate,—Cardinal,—Christ,—Maria,—God, . . .
Pompilia, will you let them murder me?

R 2

XII.

THE BOOK AND THE RING.

HERE were the end, had anything an 'end:
Thus, lit and launched, up and up roared and soared
A rocket, till the key o' the vault was reached
And wide heaven held, a breathless minute-space,
In brilliant usurpature: thus caught spark,   5
Rushéd to the height, and hung at full of fame
Over men's upturned faces, ghastly thence,
Our glaring Guido: now decline must be.
In its explosion, you have seen his act,
By my power—may-be, judged it by your own,—   10
Or composite as good orbs prove, or crammed
With worse ingredients than the Wormwood Star.
The act, over and ended, falls and fades:
What was once seen, grows what is now described,
Then talked of, told about, a tinge the less   15
In every fresh transmission; till it melts,
Trickles in silent orange or wan grey

Across our memory, dies and leaves all dark,
And presently we find the stars again.
Follow the main streaks, meditate the mode   20
Of brightness, how it hastes to blend with black !

After that February Twenty-Two,
Since our salvation, Sixteen-Ninety-Eight,
Of all reports that were, or may have been,
Concerning those the day killed or let live,   25
Four I count only.   Take the first that comes.
A letter from a stranger, man of rank,
Venetian visitor at Rome,—who knows,
On what pretence of busy idleness?
Thus he begins on evening of that day.   30

———————◆———————

" Here are we at our end of Carnival ;
" Prodigious gaiety and monstrous mirth,
" And constant shift of entertaining show :
" With influx, from each quarter of the globe,
" Of strangers nowise wishful to be last   35
" I' the struggle for a good place presently
" When that befalls fate cannot long defer.
" The old Pope totters on the verge o' the grave :
" You see, Malpichi understood far more
" Than Tozzi how to treat the ailments : age,   40
" No question, renders these inveterate.

" Cardinal Spada, actual Minister,
" Is possible Pope ; I wager on his head,
" Since those four entertainments of his niece
" Which set all Rome a-stare : Pope probably— 45
" Though Colloredo has his backers too,
" And San Cesario makes one doubt at times :
" Altieri will be Chamberlain at most.

" A week ago the sun was warm like May,
" And the old man took daily exercise   50
" Along the river-side ; he loves to see
" That Custom-house he built upon the bank,
" For, Naples born, his tastes are maritime :
" But yesterday he had to keep in-doors
" Because of the outrageous rain that fell.   55
" On such days the good soul has fainting-fits,
" Or lies in stupor, scarcely makes believe
" Of minding business, fumbles at his beads.
" They say, the trust that keeps his heart alive
" Is that, by lasting till December next,   60
" He may hold Jubilee a second time,
" And, twice in one reign, ope the Holy Doors.
" By the way, somebody responsible
" Assures me that the King of France has writ
" Fresh orders : Fénelon will be condemned :   65
" The Cardinal makes a wry face enough,

" Having a love for the delinquent : still,

" He 's the ambassador, must press the point.

" Have you a wager too, dependent here?

" Now, from such matters to divert awhile,   70

" Hear of to-day's event which crowns the week,

" Casts all the other wagers into shade.

" Tell Dandolo I owe him fifty drops

" Of heart's blood in the shape of gold zecchines !

" The Pope has done his worst : I have to pay   75

" For the execution of the Count, by Jove !

" Two days since, I reported him as safe,

" Re-echoing the conviction of all Rome :

" Who could suspect its one deaf ear—the Pope's ?

" But prejudices grow insuperable,   80

" And that old enmity to Austria, that

" Passion for France and France's pageant-king

" (Of which, why pause to multiply the proofs

" Now scandalously rife in Europe's mouth ?)

" These fairly got the better in our man   85

" Of justice, prudence, and *esprit de corps*,

" And he persisted in the butchery.

" Also, 't is said that in his latest walk

" To that Dogana-by-the-Bank he built,

" The crowd,—he suffers question, unrebuked,—

" Asked, ' Whether murder was a privilege   91

" ' Only reserved for nobles like the Count? '
" And he was ever mindful of the mob.
" Martinez, the Cæsarian Minister,
" —Who used his best endeavours to spare blood,
" And strongly pleaded for the life ' of one,'   96
" Urged he, ' I may have dined at table with ! '—
" He will not soon forget the Pope's rebuff,
" —Feels the slight sensibly, I promise you !
" And but for the dissuasion of two eyes   100
" That make with him foul weather or fine day,
" He had abstained, nor graced the spectacle :
" As it was, barely would he condescend
" Look forth from the *palchetto* where he sat
" Under the Pincian : we shall hear of this.   105
" The substituting, too, the People's Square
" For the out-o'-the-way old quarter by the Bridge,
" Was meant as a conciliatory sop
" To the mob ; it gave one holiday the more.
" But the French Embassy might unfurl flag,—   110
" Still the good luck of France to fling a foe !
" Cardinal Bouillon triumphs properly.
" *Palchetti* were erected in the Place,
" And houses, at the edge of the Three Streets,
" Let their front windows at six dollars each :   115
" Anguisciola, that patron of the arts,
" Hired one ; our Envoy Contarini too.

" Now for the thing; no sooner the decree
" Gone forth,—'t is four-and-twenty hours ago,—
" Than Acciaiuoli and Panciatichi,   120
" Old friends, indeed compatriots of the man,
" Being pitched on as the couple properest
" To intimate the sentence yesternight,
" Were closeted ere cock-crow with the Count.
" They both report their efforts to dispose   125
" The unhappy nobleman for ending well,
" Despite the natural sense of injury,
" Were crowned at last with a complete success.
" And when the Company of Death arrived
" At twenty-hours,—the way they reckon here,—   130
" We say, at sunset, after dinner-time,—
" The Count was led down, hoisted up on car,
" Last of the five, as heinousest, you know :
" Yet they allowed one whole car to each man.
" His intrepidity, nay, nonchalance,   135
" As up he stood and down he sat himself,
" Struck admiration into those who saw.
" Then the procession started, took the way
" From the New Prisons by the Pilgrim's Street,
" The street of the Governo, Pasquin's Street,   140
" (Where was stuck up, mid other epigrams,
" A quatrain . . . but of all that, presently !)
" The Place Navona, the Pantheon's Place,

" Place of the Column, last the Corso's length,
" And so debouched thence at Mannaia's foot   145
" I' the Place o' the People.   As is evident,
" (Despite the malice,—plainly meant, I fear,
" By this abrupt change of locality,—
" The Square 's no such bad place to head and hang)
" We had the titillation as we sat   150
" Assembled, (quality in conclave, ha ?)
" Of, minute after minute, some report
" How the slow show was winding on its way.
" Now did a car run over, kill a man,
" Just opposite a pork-shop numbered Twelve :   155
" And bitter were the outcries of the mob
" Against the Pope : for, but that he forbids
" The Lottery, why, Twelve were Tern Quatern !
" Now did a beggar by Saint Agnes, lame
" From his youth up, recover use of leg,   160
" Through prayer of Guido as he glanced that way :
" So that the crowd near crammed his hat with coin.
" Thus was kept up excitement to the last,
" —Not an abrupt out-bolting, as of yore,
" From Castle, over Bridge and on to block,   165
" And so all ended ere you well could wink !

" To mount the scaffold-steps, Guido was last
" Here also, as atrociousest in crime.

" We hardly noticed how the peasants died,

" They dangled somehow soon to right and left,   170

" And we remained all ears and eyes, could give

" Ourselves to Guido undividedly,

" As he harangued the multitude beneath.

" He begged forgiveness on the part of God,

" And fair construction of his act from men,   175

" Whose suffrage he entreated for his soul,

" Suggesting that we should forthwith repeat

" A *Pater* and an *Ave*, with the hymn

" *Salve Regina Cœli*, for his sake.

" Which said, he turned to the confessor, crossed

" And reconciled himself, with decency,   181

" Oft glancing at Saint Mary's opposite,

" Where they possess, and showed in shrine to-day,

" The blessed *Umbilicus* of our Lord,

" (A relic 't is believed no other church   185

" In Rome can boast of)—then rose up, as brisk

" Knelt down again, bent head, adapted neck,

" And, with the name of Jesus on his lips,

" Received the fatal blow.

                      " The headsman showed

" The head to the populace.   Must I avouch   191

" We strangers own to disappointment here ?

" Report pronounced him fully six feet high,

" Youngish, considering his fifty years,
" And, if not handsome, dignified at least.   195
" Indeed, it was no face to please a wife !
" His friends say, this was caused by the costume :
" He wore the dress he did the murder in,
" That is, a *just-a-corps* of russet serge,
" Black camisole, coarse cloak of baracan   200
" (So they style here the garb of goat's-hair cloth)
" White hat and cotton cap beneath, poor Count
" Preservative against the evening dews
" During the journey from Arezzo.   Well,
" So died the man, and so his end was peace ;   205
" Whence many a moral were to meditate.
" Spada,—you may bet Dandolo,—is Pope !
" Now for the quatrain ! "

No, friend, this will do !
You 've sputtered into sparks.   What streak comes next ?
A letter : Don Giacinto Arcangeli,   211
Doctor and Proctor, him I made you mark
Buckle to business in his study late,
The virtuous sire, the valiant for the truth,
Acquaints his correspondent,—Florentine,   215
By name Cencini, advocate as well,
Socius and brother-in-the-devil to match,—

A friend of Franceschini, anyhow,
And knit up with the bowels of the case,—
Acquaints him, (in this paper that I touch)   220
How their joint effort to obtain reprieve
For Guido had so nearly nicked the nine
And ninety and one over,—folk would say
At Tarocs,—or succeeded,—in our phrase.
To this Cencini's care I owe the Book,.   225
The yellow thing I take and toss once more,—
How will it be, my four-years'-intimate,
When thou and I part company anon ?—
'T was he, the " whole position of the case,"
Pleading and summary, were put before ;   230
Discreetly in my Book he bound them all,
Adding some three epistles to the point.
Here is the first of these, part fresh as penned,
The sand, that dried the ink, not rubbed away,
Though penned the day whereof it tells the deed :
Part—extant just as plainly, you know where,   236
Whence came the other stuff, went, you know how,
To make the Ring that 's all but round and done.

———————

" Late they arrived, too late, egregious Sir,
" Those same justificative points you urge   240
" Might benefit His Blessed Memory

" Count Guido Franceschini now with God :
" Since the Court,—to state things succinctly,—styled
" The Congregation of the Governor,
" Having resolved on Tuesday last our cause   245
" I' the guilty sense, with death for punishment,
" Spite of all pleas by me deducible
" In favour of said Blessed Memory,—
" I, with expenditure of pains enough,
" Obtained a respite, leave to claim and prove   250
" Exemption from the law's award,—alleged
" The power and privilege o' the Clericate :
" To which effect a courier was despatched.
" But ere an answer from Arezzo came,
" The Holiness of our Lord the Pope (prepare !)   255
" Judging it inexpedient to postpone
" The execution of such sentence passed,
" Saw fit, by his particular cheirograph,
" To derogate, dispense with privilege,
" And wink at any hurt accruing thence   260
" To Mother Church through damage of her son :
" Also, to overpass and set aside
" That other plea on score of tender age,
" Put forth by me to do Pasquini good,
" One of the four in trouble with our friend.   265
" So that all five, to-day, have suffered death
" With no distinction save in dying,—he,

" Decollate by mere due of privilege,
" The rest hanged decently and in order.   Thus
" Came the Count to his end of gallant man,   270
" Defunct in faith and exemplarity :
" Nor shall the shield of his great House lose shine
" Thereby, nor its blue banner blush to red.
" This, too, should yield sustainment to our hearts—
" He had commiseration and respect   275
" In his decease from universal Rome,
" *Quantum est hominum venustiorum,*
" The nice and cultivated everywhere :
" Though, in respect of me his advocate,
" Needs must I groan o'er my debility,   280
" Attribute the untoward event o' the strife
" To nothing but my own crass ignorance
" Which failed to set the valid reasons forth,
" Find fit excuse : such is the fate of war !
" May God compensate us the direful blow   285
" By future blessings on his family,
" Whereof I lowly beg the next commands ;
" —Whereto, as humbly, I confirm myself . . . ."

And so forth,—follow name and place and date.
On next leaf—   290
                " *Hactenus senioribus !*
" There, old fox, show the clients t' other side

" And keep this corner sacred, I beseech !
" You and your pleas and proofs were what folk call
" Pisan assistance, aid that comes too late,   295
" Saves a man dead as nail in post of door.
" Had I but time and space for narrative !
" What was the good of twenty Clericates
" When Somebody's thick headpiece once was bent
" On seeing Guido's drop into the bag?   300
" How these old men like giving youth a push !
" So much the better : next push goes to him,
" And a new Pope begins the century.
" Much good I get by my superb defence !
" But argument is solid and subsists,   305
" While obstinacy and ineptitude
" Accompany the owner to his tomb—
" What do I care how soon?   Beside, folk see !
" Rome will have relished heartily the show,
" Yet understood the motives, never fear,   310
" Which caused the indecent change o' the People's
        Place
" To the People's Playground,—stigmatize the spite
" Which in a trice precipitated things !
" As oft the moribund will give a kick
" To show they are not absolutely dead,   315
" So feebleness i' the socket shoots its last,
" A spirt of violence for energy !

" But thou, Cencini, brother of my breast,
" O fox whose home is 'mid the tender grape,
" Whose couch in Tuscany by Themis' throne,   320
" Subject to no such . . . best I shut my mouth
" Or only open it again to say,
" This pother and confusion fairly laid,
" My hands are empty and my satchel lank.
" Now then for both the Matrimonial Cause   325
" And the Case of Gomez! Serve them hot and hot!

" *Reliqua differamus in crastinum!*
" The impatient estafette cracks whip outside :
" Still, though the earth should swallow him who swears
" And me who make the mischief, in must slip—   330
" My boy, your godson, fat-chaps Hyacinth,
" Enjoyed the sight while Papa plodded here.
" I promised him, the rogue, a month ago,
" The day his birthday was, of all the days,
" That if I failed to save Count Guido's head,   335
" Cinuccio should at least go see it chopped
" From trunk—' So, latinize your thanks! quoth I.
" ' That I prefer, *hoc malim,*' raps me out
" The rogue : you notice the subjunctive? Ah !
" Accordingly he sat there, bold in box,   340
" Proud as the Pope behind the peacock-fans :
" Whereon a certain lady-patroness

X.   S

" For whom I manage things (my boy in front,

" Her Marquis sat the third in evidence;

" Boys have no eyes nor ears save for the show)   345

" ' This time, Cintino,' was her sportive word,

" When whiz and thump went axe and mowed lay man,

" And folk could fall to the suspended chat,

" ' This time, you see, Bottini rules the roast,

" ' Nor can Papa with all his eloquence   350

" ' Be reckoned on to help as heretofore ! '

" Whereat Cinone pouts ; then, sparkishly—

" ' Papa knew better than aggrieve his Pope,

" ' And baulk him of his grudge against our Count,

" ' Else he 'd have argued-off Bottini's ' . . what? 355

" ' His nose,'—the rogue ! well parried of the boy !

" He 's long since out of Cæsar (eight years old)

" And as for tripping in Eutropius . . . well,

" Reason the more that we strain every nerve

" To do him justice, mould a model-mouth,   360

" A Bartolus-cum-Baldo for next age :

" For that I purse the pieces, work the brain,

" And want both Gomez and the marriage-case,

" Success with which shall plaster aught of pate

" That 's broken in me by Bottini's flail,   365

" And bruise his own, belike, that wags and brags.

" *Adverti supplico humiliter*

·   " *Quod* don't the fungus see, the fop divine

" That one hand drives two horses, left and right?
" With this rein did I rescue from the ditch   370
" The fortune of our Franceschini, keep
" Unsplashed the credit of a noble House,
" And set the fashionable cause at Rome
" A-prancing till bystanders shouted ''ware !'
" The other rein's judicious management   375
" Suffered old Somebody to keep the pace,
" Hobblingly play the roadster : who but he
" Had his opinion, was not led by the nose
" In leash of quibbles strung to look like law !
" You 'll soon see,—when I go to pay devoir   380
" And compliment him on confuting me,—
" If, by a back-swing of the pendulum,
" Grace be not, thick and threefold, consequent.
" ' I must decide as I see proper, Don !
" ' I 'm Pope, I have my inward lights for guide.   385
" ' Had learning been the matter in dispute,
" ' Could eloquence avail to gainsay fact,
" ' Yours were the victory, be comforted !'
" Cinuzzo will be gainer by it all.
" Quick then with Gomez, hot and hot next case !"

Follows, a letter, takes the other side.   391
Tall blue-eyed Fisc whose head is capped with cloud,

Doctor Bottini,—to no matter who,
Writes on the Monday two days afterward.
Now shall the honest championship of right,   395
Crowned with success, enjoy at last, unblamed,
Moderate triumph !   Now shall eloquence
Poured forth in fancied floods for virtue's sake,
(The print is sorrowfully dyked and dammed,
But shows where fain the unbridled force would flow,
Finding a channel)—now shall this refresh   401
The thirsty donor with a drop or two !
Here has been truth at issue with a lie :
Let who gained truth the day have handsome pride
In his own prowess !   Eh !   What ails the man?   405

———————

" Well, it is over, ends as I foresaw :
" Easily proved, Pompilia's innocence !
" Catch them entrusting Guido's guilt to me
" Who had, as usual, the plain truth to plead.
" I always knew the clearness of the stream   410
" Would show the fish so thoroughly, child might prong
" The clumsy monster : with no mud to splash,
" Small credit to lynx-eye and lightning-spear !
" This Guido,—(much sport he contrived to make,
" Who at .irst twist, preamble of the cord,   415
" Turned white, told all, like the poltroon he was !) —

" Finished, as you expect, a penitent,
" Fully confessed his crime, and made amends,
" And, edifying Rome last Saturday,
" Died like a saint, poor devil ! That 's the man 420
" The gods still give to my antagonist :
" Imagine how Arcangeli claps wing
" And crows ! ' Such formidable facts to face,
" ' So naked to attack, my client here,
" ' And yet I kept a month the Fisc at bay, 425
" ' And in the end had foiled him of the prize
" ' By this arch-stroke, this plea of privilege,
" ' But that the Pope must gratify his whim,
" ' Put in his word, poor old man,—let it pass !'
" —Such is the cue to which all Rome responds. 430
" What with the plain truth given me to uphold,
" And, should I let truth slip, the Pope at hand
" To pick up, steady her on legs again,
" My office turns a pleasantry indeed !
" Not that the burly boaster did one jot 435
" O' the little was to do—young Spreti's work !
" But for him,—mannikin and dandiprat,
" Mere candle-end and inch of cleverness
" Stuck on Arcangeli's save-all,—but for him 439
" The spruce young Spreti, what is bad were worse !

" I looked that Rome should have the natural gird

" At advocate with case that proves itself;
" I knew Arcangeli would grin and brag :
" But what say you to one impertinence
" Might move a stone ? That monk, you are to know,
" That barefoot Augustinian whose report   446
" O' the dying woman's words did detriment
" To my best points it took the freshness from,
" —That meddler preached to purpose yesterday
" At San Lorenzo as a winding-up   450
" O' the show which proved a treasure to the church.
" Out comes his sermon smoking from the press :
" Its text—' Let God be true, and every man
" ' A liar '—and its application, this
" The longest-winded of the paragraphs,   455
" I straight unstitch, tear out and treat you with :
" 'T is piping hot and posts through Rome to-day.
" Remember it, as I engage to do !

" But if you rather be disposed to see
" In the result of the long trial here,—   460
" This dealing doom to guilt and doling praise
" To innocency,—any proof that truth
" May look for vindication from the world,
" Much will you have misread the signs, I say.
" God, who seems acquiescent in the main   465

" With those who add ' So will he ever sleep '—
" Flutters their foolishness from time to time,
" Puts forth His right-hand recognizably;
" Even as, to fools who deem He needs must right
" Wrong on the instant, as if earth were heaven,   470
" He wakes remonstrance—' Passive, Lord, how long?'
" Because Pompilia's purity prevails,
" Conclude you, all truth triumphs in the end?
" So might those old inhabitants of the ark,
" Witnessing haply their dove's safe return,   475
" Pronounce there was no danger, all the while
" O' the deluge, to the creature's counterparts,
" Aught that beat wing i' the world, was white or soft,—
" And that the lark, the thrush, the culver too,
" Might equally have traversed air, found earth,   480
" And brought back olive-branch in unharmed bill.
" Methinks I hear the Patriarch's warning voice—
" ' Though this one breast, by miracle, return,
" ' No wave rolls by, in all the waste, but bears
" ' Within it some dead dove-like thing as dear,   485
" ' Beauty made blank and harmlessness destroyed!'
" How many chaste and noble sister-fames
" Wanted the extricating hand, so lie
" Strangled, for one Pompilia proud above
" The welter, plucked from the world's calumny,   490
" Stupidity, simplicity,—who cares?

" Romans !   An elder race possessed your land
" Long ago, and a false faith lingered still,
" As shades do though the morning-star be out.
" Doubtless some pagan of the twilight-day   495
" Has often pointed to a cavern-mouth
" Obnoxious to beholders, hard by Rome,
" And said,—nor he a bad man, no, nor fool,
" Only a man born blind like all his mates,—
" ' Here skulk in safety, lurk, defying law,   500
" ' The devotees to execrable creed,
" ' Adoring—with what culture . . . Jove, avert
" ' Thy vengeance from us worshippers of thee ! . . .
" ' What rites obscene—their idol-god, an Ass !'
" So went the word forth, so acceptance found,   505
" So century re-echoed century,
" Cursed the accursed,—and so, from sire to son,
" You Romans cried ' The offscourings of our race
" ' Corrupt within the depths there : fitly fiends
" ' Perform a temple-service o'er the dead :   510
" ' Child, gather garment round thee, pass nor pry !'
" Thus groaned your generations : till the time
" Grew ripe, and lightning had revealed, belike,—
" Thro' crevice peeped into by curious fear,—
" Some object even fear could recognize   515
" I' the place of spectres ; on the illumined wall,
" To-wit, some nook, tradition talks about,

" Narrow and short, a corpse's length, no more :

" And by it, in the due receptacle,

" The little rude brown lamp of earthenware,　520

" The cruse, was meant for flowers but now held blood,

" The rough-scratched palm-branch, and the legend left

" *Pro Christo.*　Then the mystery lay clear :

" The abhorred one was a martyr all the time,

" Heaven's saint whereof earth was not worthy.　What ?

" Do you continue in the old belief ?　526

" Where blackness bides unbroke, must devils brood ?

" Is it so certain not another cell

" O' the myriad that make up the catacomb

" Contains some saint a second flash would show ?　530

" Will you ascend into the light of day

" And, having recognized a martyr's shrine,

" Go join the votaries that gape around

" Each vulgar god that awes the market-place ?

" Are these the objects of your praising ?　See !　535

" In the outstretched right hand of Apollo, there,

" Lies screened a scorpion :　housed amid the folds

" Of Juno's mantle lurks a centipede !

" Each statue of a god were fitlier styled

" Demon and devil.　Glorify no brass　540

" That shines like burnished gold in noonday glare,

" For fools !　Be otherwise instructed, you !

" And preferably ponder, ere ye judge,

" Each incident of this strange human play
" Privily acted on a theatre   545
" That seemed secure from every gaze but God's,—
" Till, of a sudden, earthquake laid wall low
" And let the world perceive wild work inside
" And how, in petrifaction of surprise,
" The actors stood,—raised arm and planted foot,—
" Mouth as it made, eye as it evidenced,   551
" Despairing shriek, triumphant hate,—transfixed,
" Both he who takes and she who yields the life.

" As ye become spectators of this scene,
" Watch obscuration of a pearl-pure fame   555
" By vapoury films, enwoven circumstance,
" —A soul made weak by its pathetic want
" Of just the first apprenticeship to sin
" Which thenceforth makes the sinning soul secure
" From all foes save itself, souls' truliest foe,—   560
" Since egg turned snake needs fear no serpentry,—
" As ye behold this web of circumstance
" Deepen the more for every thrill and throe,
" Convulsive effort to disperse the films
" And disenmesh the fame o' the martyr,—mark   565
" How all those means, the unfriended one pursues,
" To keep the treasure trusted to her breast,
" Each struggle in the flight from death to life,

" How all, by procuration of the powers
" Of darkness, are transformed,—no single ray,   570
" Shot forth to show and save the inmost star,
" But, passed as through hell's prism, proceeding black
" To the world that hates white : as ye watch, I say,
" Till dusk and such defacement grow eclipse
" By,—marvellous perversity of man !—   575
" The inadequacy and inaptitude
" Of that self-same machine, that very law
" Man vaunts, devised to dissipate the gloom,
" Rescue the drowning orb from calumny,
" —Hear law, appointed to defend the just,   580
" Submit, for best defence, that wickedness
" Was bred of flesh and innate with the bone
" Borne by Pompilia's spirit for a space,
" And no mere chance fault, passionate and brief :
" Finally, when ye find,—after this touch   585
" Of man's protection which intends to mar
" The last pin-point of light and damn the disc,—
" One wave of the hand of God amid the worlds
" Bid vapour vanish, darkness flee away,
" And let the vexed star culminate in peace   590
" Approachable no more by earthly mist—
" What I call God's hand,—you, perhaps,—mere chance
" Of the true instinct of an old good man
" Who happens to hate darkness and love light,—

" In whom too was the eye that saw, not dim,   595
" The natural force to do the thing he saw,
" Nowise abated,—both by miracle,—
" All this well pondered,—I demand assent
" To the enunciation of my text
" In face of one proof more that ' God is true   600
" ' And every man a liar '—that who trusts
" To human testimony for a fact
" Gets this sole fact—himself is proved a fool ;
" Man's speech being false, if but by consequence
" That only strength is true : while man is weak,   605
" And, since truth seems reserved for heaven not earth,
" Plagued here by earth's prerogative of lies,
" Should learn to love and long for what, one day,
" Approved by life's probation, he may speak.

" For me, the weary and worn, who haply prompt 610
" To mirth or pity, as I move the mood,—
" A friar who glides unnoticed to the grave,
" With these bare feet, coarse robe and rope-girt waist,—
" I have long since renounced your world, ye know :
" Yet what forbids I weigh the prize forgone,   615
" The worldly worth?   I dare, as I were dead,
" Disinterestedly judge this and that
" Good ye account good : but God tries the heart.
" Still, if you question me of my content

" At having put each human pleasure by,   620

" I answer, at the urgency of truth :

" As this world seems, I dare not say I know

" —Apart from Christ's assurance which decides—

" Whether I have not failed to taste much joy.

" For many a doubt will fain perturb my choice—

" Many a dream of life spent otherwise—   626

" How human love, in varied shapes, might work

" As glory, or as rapture, or as grace :

" How conversancy with the books that teach,

" The arts that help,— how, to grow good and great,

" Rather than simply good, and bring thereby   631

" Goodness to breathe and live, nor, born i' the brain,

" Die there,—how these and many another gift

" Of life are precious though abjured by me.

" But, for one prize, best meed of mightiest man,

" Arch-object of ambition,—earthly praise,   636

" Repute o' the world, the flourish of loud trump,

" The softer social fluting,—Oh, for these,

" —No, my friends !   Fame,—that bubble which, world-wide

" Each blows and bids his neighbour lend a breath,

" That so he haply may behold thereon   641

" One more enlarged distorted false fool's-face,

" Until some glassy nothing grown as big

" Send by a touch the imperishable to suds,—

"No, in renouncing fame, my loss was light,   645
"Choosing obscurity, my chance was well!"

Didst ever touch such ampollosity
As the monk's own bubble, let alone its spite?
What's his speech for, but just the fame he flouts?
How he dares reprehend both high and low,   650
Nor stoops to turn the sentence "God is true
"And every man a liar—save the Pope
"Happily reigning—my respects to him!"
And so round off the period.   Molinism
Simple and pure!   To what pitch get we next?   655
I find that, for first pleasant consequence,
Gomez, who had intended to appeal
From the absurd decision of the Court,
Declines, though plain enough his privilege,
To call on help from lawyers any more—   660
Resolves earth's liars may possess the world
Till God have had sufficiency of both:
So may I whistle for my job and fee!

But, for this virulent and rabid monk,—
If law be an inadequate machine,   665
And advocacy, froth and impotence,
We shall soon see, my blatant brother!   That's

Exactly what I hope to show your sort !
For, by a veritable piece of luck,
The providence, you monks round period with, 670
All may be gloriously retrieved. Perpend!
That Monastery of the Convertites
Whereto the Court consigned Pompilia first,
—Observe, if convertite, why, sinner then,
Or what's the pertinency of award ?— 675
And whither she was late returned to die,
—Still in their jurisdiction, mark again !—
That thrifty Sisterhood, for perquisite,
Claims every piece whereof may die possessed
Each sinner in the circuit of its walls. 680
Now, this Pompilia seeing that, by death
O' the couple, all their wealth devolved on her,
Straight utilized the respite ere decease,
By regular conveyance of the goods
She thought her own, to will and to devise,— 685
Gave all to friends, Tighetti and the like,
In trust for him she held her son and heir,
Gaetano,—trust which ends with infancy :
So willing and devising, since assured
The justice of the Court would presently 690
Confirm her in her rights and exculpate,
Re-integrate and rehabilitate—
Place her as, through my pleading, now she stands.

But here 's the capital mistake : the Court
Found Guido guilty,—but pronounced no word   695
About the innocency of his wife :
I grounded charge on broader base, I hope !
No matter whether wife be true or false,
The husband must not push aside the law,
And punish of a sudden : that 's the point :   700
Gather from out my speech the contrary !
It follows that Pompilia, unrelieved
By formal sentence from imputed fault,
Remains unfit to have and to dispose
Of property which law provides shall lapse.   705
Wherefore the Monastery claims its due :
And whose, pray, whose the office, but the Fisc's ?
Who but I institute procedure next
Against the person of dishonest life,
Pompilia whom last week I sainted so ?   710
I. it is teach the monk what scripture means,
And that the tongue should prove a two-edged sword,
No axe sharp one side, blunt the other way,
Like what amused the town at Guido's cost !
Astræa redux ! I 've a second chance   715
Before the self-same Court o' the Governor
Who soon shall see volte-face and chop, change sides.
Accordingly, I charge you on your life,
Send me with all despatch the judgment late

O' the Florence Rota Court, confirmative   720
O' the prior judgment at Arezzo, clenched
Again by the Granducal signature,
Wherein Pompilia is convicted, doomed,
And only destined to escape through flight
The proper punishment.   Send me the piece,—   725
I 'll work it !   And this foul-mouthed friar shall find
His Noah's-dove that brought the olive back
Turn into quite the other sooty scout,
The raven, Noah first put forth the ark,
Which never came back but ate carcasses !   730
No adequate machinery in law ?
No power of life and death i' the learned tongue ?
Methinks I am already at my speech,
Startle the world with "Thou, Pompilia, thus ?
"How is the fine gold of the Temple dim !"   735
And so forth.   But the courier bids me close,
And clip away one joke that runs through Rome,
Side by side with the sermon which I send.
How like the heartlessness of the old hunks
Arcangeli !   His Count is hardly cold,   740
The client whom his blunders sacrificed,
When somebody must needs describe the scene—
How the procession ended at the church
That boasts the famous relic : quoth our brute,
"Why, that 's just Martial's phrase for ' make an end '—
    X.   T

" Ad umbilicum sic perventum est ! "   746
The callous dog,—let who will cut off head,
He cuts a joke and cares no more than so !
I think my speech shall modify his mirth.
" How is the fine gold dim ! "—but send the piece !

Alack, Bottini, what is my next word   751
But death to all that hope ?   The Instrument
Is plain before me, print that ends my Book
With the definitive verdict of the Court,
Dated September, six months afterward,   755
(Such trouble and so long the old Pope gave !)
" In restitution of the perfect fame
" Of dead Pompilia, *quondam* Guido's wife,
" And warrant to her representative
" Domenico Tighetti, barred hereby,   760
" While doing duty in his guardianship,
" From all molesting, all disquietude,
" Each perturbation and vexation brought
" Or threatened to be brought against the heir
" By the Most Venerable Convent called   765
" Saint Mary Magdalen o' the Convertites
' I' the Corso."
                    Justice done a second time !
Well judged, Marc Antony, *Locum-tenens*

O' the Governor, a Venturini too ! 770
For which I save thy name,—last of the list !

Next year but one, completing his nine years
Of rule in Rome, died Innocent my Pope
—By some account, on his accession-day.
If he thought doubt would do the next age good,
'T is pity he died unapprised what birth 776
His reign may boast of, be remembered by—
Terrible Pope, too, of a kind,—Voltaire.

And so an end of all i' the story.   Strain
Never so much my eyes, I miss the mark 780
If lived or died that Gaetano, child
Of Guido and Pompilia : only find,
Immediately upon his father's death,
A record, in the annals of the town—
That Porzia, sister of our Guido, moved 785
The Priors of Arezzo and their head
Its Gonfalonier to give loyally
A public attestation of the right
O' the Franceschini to all reverence—
Apparently because of the incident 790
O' the murder,—there 's no mention made o' the crime,
But what else could have caused such urgency
To cure the mob, just then, of greediness

For scandal, love of lying vanity,
And appetite to swallow crude reports   795
That bring annoyance to their betters?—bane
Which, here, was promptly met by antidote.
I like and shall translate the eloquence
Of nearly the worst Latin ever writ :
" Since antique time whereof the memory   800
" Holds the beginning, to this present hour,
" The Franceschini ever shone, and shine
" Still i' the primary rank, supreme amid
" The lustres of Arezzo, proud to own
" In this great family, the flag-bearer,   805
" Guide of her steps and guardian against foe,—
" As in the first beginning, so to-day ! "
There, would you disbelieve the annalist,
Go rather by the babble of a bard?
I thought, Arezzo, thou hadst fitter souls,   810
Petrarch,—nay, Buonarroti at a pinch,
To do thee credit as *vexillifer!*
Was it mere mirth the Patavinian meant,
Making thee out, in his veracious page,
Founded by Janus of the Double Face?   815

Well, proving of such perfect parentage,
Our Gaetano, born of love and hate,
Did the babe live or die ?   I fain would find !

What were his fancies if he grew a man?
Was he proud,—a true scion of the stock   820
Which bore the blazon, shall make bright my page—
Shield, Azure, on a Triple Mountain, Or,
A Palm-tree, Proper, whereunto is tied
A Greyhound, Rampant, striving in the slips?
Or did he love his mother, the base-born,   825
And fight i' the ranks, unnoticed by the world?

Such, then, the final state o' the story. So
Did the Star Wormwood in a blazing fall
Frighten awhile the waters and lie lost.
So did this old woe fade from memory: 830
Till after, in the fulness of the days,
I needs must find an ember yet unquenched,
And, breathing, blow the spark to flame. It lives,
If precious be the soul of man to man.

So, British Public, who may like me yet,   835
(Marry and amen!) learn one lesson hence
Of many which whatever lives should teach:
This lesson, that our human speech is naught,
Our human testimony false, our fame
And human estimation words and wind.   840
Why take the artistic way to prove so much?
Because, it is the glory and good of Art,

That Art remains the one way possible
Of speaking truth, to mouths like mine at least.
How look a brother in the face and say　　　845
" Thy right is wrong, eyes hast thou yet art blind.
" Thine ears are stuffed and stopped, despite their
　　length :
" And, oh, the foolishness thou countest faith ! "
Say this as silverly as tongue can troll—
The anger of the man may be endured,　　　850
The shrug, the disappointed eyes of him
Are not so bad to bear—but here 's the plague
That all this trouble comes of telling truth,
Which truth, by when it reaches him, looks false,
Seems to be just the thing it would supplant,　　　855
Nor recognizable by whom it left :
While falsehood would have done the work of truth.
But Art,—wherein man nowise speaks to men,
Only to mankind,—Art may tell a truth
Obliquely, do the thing shall breed the thought,　　860
Nor wrong the thought, missing the mediate word.
So may you paint your picture, twice show truth,
Beyond mere imagery on the wall,—
So, note by note, bring music from your mind,
Deeper than ever e'en Beethoven dived,—　　　865
So write a book shall mean beyond the facts,
Suffice the eye and save the soul beside.

And save the soul! If this intent save mine,—
If the rough ore be rounded to a ring,
Render all duty which good ring should do,   870
And, failing grace, succeed in guardianship,—
Might mine but lie outside thine, Lyric Love,
Thy rare gold ring of verse (the poet praised)
Linking our England to his Italy!

THE TENTH VOLUME.

PRINTED BY
SPOTTISWOODE AND CO., NEW-STREET SQUARE
LONDON